Enjo
Jackie Zack

An Irish
Heart

Jackie Zack

ISBN-13: 978-1507771020
ISBN-10: 1507771029

Dedicated to you, the reader. ☺

ACKNOWLEDGMENTS

Thank you to my wonderful family, friends, and ACFW
critique group. All of you are the best.

As you slide down the banister of life, may the splinters never point the wrong direction.

Irish Proverb

Chapter 1

"Go to Cork." The light blue eyes of her mother beckoned.

Greta struggled to understand the words as Aunt Sophie took her hand and led her into the hallway. She didn't want to leave and glanced back to see Dad stepping close to Mom's bedside.

"What did mommy mean? Why'd she say that?"

"Greta, your mommy didn't say anything. She's been in a coma. You know what that is, right?"

She nodded in answer. "But she did speak to me. She looked at me and told me to go to Cork."

"No, honey." Her aunt bent down to Greta's eye level. "She's in heaven now."

"Where is Cork?" *Is heaven—Cork?*

"It's a county in Ireland. County Cork. Your mother lived there for a while."

The memory of the scene seemed as vivid as if it happened yesterday. But her mom had passed away twenty-two years ago when Greta was five. She sighed and her eyes brimmed with tears. Losing her mother had been like losing her own life.

Replaying the thoughts in her mind was inevitable as she drove the small rental car away from Cork City airport. Her arms trembled, but strength rose within. Her mom wanted her to journey here—where Mom met Dad.

Greta took a deep breath of cool late-summer air and reminded herself to keep to the left of the road. Cork City was a colorful mix of new and old with many places to explore. But finding a smaller town to set up as home-base suited her. Once she had the idea, nothing else seemed right.

The foreign countryside beckoned to her like a haunting Celtic song. The rolling green fields marked with a narrow road ahead and backlit by the low evening sun was surreal.

Driving further, her car was the only one on the road which added to the eerie quality. She seemed to travel on the edge of the world—everything else slipped further away from her. What if her car died? How long would it be before someone found her?

Her imagination supplied her with wild thoughts of a murderer crossing her path. He'd be a crazy character with pasty skin, greasy hair and a wicked knife. She'd do her best to run away or kick and fight, but her younger brother and father would never see her again.

She gripped the steering wheel harder. Bart and Dad would be fine. They were busy with their own lives anyway. She had no other choice than to come. The image of her mom's beautiful face came to mind again. "Go to Cork."

Besides that, she trusted she'd be fine. When her imagination showed her tragic scenarios, it was always wrong. When Dad was late coming home, he was never in an auto accident and barely hanging on to life. And when her little brother at the age of three had disappeared for half a day, he hadn't been kidnapped. He'd fallen asleep in the closet under an old coat.

So why worry about the worst case scenario? She'd already done her share of worrying and needed to focus on positive things.

After navigating tight turns and passing through some small points of civilization consisting of a few buildings and a petrol station, a moderately-sized village came into view. The sea sparkled behind it, and the sun nearly touched the glassy horizon. Choosing a place so soon wasn't something she planned to do, but its name, Angel's Hollow, touched her heart. She needed God's comfort and help.

A red house gave way to rows of brightly colored shops built right next to each other. The striking colors were probably a way to define where one stopped and the other started—dark green, canary yellow, periwinkle blue, maraschino cherry red, and cotton candy pink.

Finding an open space on the side of the road, Greta parked and stepped out of the car to get a closer look at the businesses. The brick sidewalks and flower boxes added to the riot of color. She loved the gift shops—especially the ones with rich-looking crystal and earthy pottery. Nearby a bakery showcased cupcakes and scones. Across the street were a couple of pubs and an enticing restaurant or two.

Couples strode by her, talking animatedly. Tourists. Some of the languages she couldn't quite determine. Had to be a European dialect. Another group was American with a New York accent. The family wore their wealth well with immaculate clothing and strode by with an air of importance. She lost interest in them as a man about her age headed toward her.

He walked in a hurried pace, holding a bouquet of red and white carnations. She almost forgot how to breathe. The woman who was to receive those flowers had to be the luckiest one on earth. His dark hair, friendly face, and lean build were everything she admired in a man, right down to his neatly trimmed facial hair.

He looked directly at her, his blue-gray eyes widening in the process. He took a nasty stumble, but righted himself in the next stride. As he neared, he studied her face, then stopped in front of her. His forehead wrinkled. "Iona?"

"Sorry. You must have me confused with another." Greta used her much-practiced Irish accent.

His mouth dropped open and his eyes became wary. She moved to pass by, but he stopped her with a light touch on her sleeve. "You're not? But you look exactly like me ex—you're codding."

"Cod? Fish?" The words slipped out without the added accent. No, not fish. Codding... it meant kidding. Didn't do too well with that one, but at least it finally came to her.

"If you don't mind me asking, where're you from?" The bouquet took a downward turn and languished by his leg.

"The Midwest." She tried the accent again.

"The Midwest, aye?" He scratched his beard. "Westmeath? Offaly? Galway?"

She shook her head at each one. "Indiana."

His puzzled look and defeated manner of lifting his shoulders to let them drop made her smile.

"Oh. That there. You're definitely not Iona." He smiled back. "You're from the States then? Indiana must be one of the fifty?"

"Yes."

"Gave me quite a turn. Will you be here for a while?"

She nodded.

"Stop by O'Riain's Cottage," he pointed to the pink hotel with a restaurant across the street, "and I'll get you a glass. I'm Aedan. Aedan O'Riain."

"I'm Greta Conner."

He seemed to force a smile as he nodded and turned to leave. What was so odd about her name?

****

Aedan rushed across the street to O'Riain's Cottage without a backward glance. Her last words telling him that she was Greta Conner floated through his head. How did Iona think she could fool him like that? What was her plan? To humiliate him again?

He handed his mother the carnations. "Happy birthday, Ma."

She took the bouquet and slapped his shoulder with it. "Funny. I get the same joke every week. At that rate, I'll be five-hundred years old. What are you going to get for me real birthday?"

"Carnations."

"I thought so." She sighed and began to fill the vases, each with a single flower for the café tables.

Aedan headed to the kitchen to help his little brother. He really shouldn't think of him as little anymore. Reece was twenty-eight, a year younger than himself, plus they were of equal height. People who didn't know them well would often mistake one for the other. What a bother.

Reece submerged sliced potatoes in boiling oil. "It's about time you got here. I'm off."

"No, you don't. A big group walked in." Aedan grabbed a pencil and tablet to take their order.

"You don't need me here." Reece crossed his arms over his chest. "What with Liam and Ma."

"Liam's scheduled to leave early. Remember? His wife had a baby."

"Brutal." Reece plopped raw fish fillets into flour.

Aedan smiled. He wasn't sure if his brother referred to having to stay later or Liam's baby. He

8

couldn't wait to see his expression when Iona walked in the door. That is, if she'd come. In the back of his mind he supposed it could be possible that she wasn't Iona and was in fact Greta Conner as she introduced herself. Aye, right.

After forty-five minutes of eyeing the clock and the front entrance, he wasn't disappointed. The redheaded arrived.

In her favor, she surveyed her surroundings in a wide-eyed disoriented manner, and then sat at a table for two. She bent forward and smelled the red carnation. Either she was from the States, or Iona had become the actress she'd set out to be.

Her gaze didn't turn his direction, so he hurried to the kitchen.

"You have to see who walked in." Aedan frowned at his brother's flour covered hands. "Quick, wash that off."

"Who?" He chuckled. "Is it that old peeler again with the gammy leg?"

An image of the older policeman in shorts with one normal leg and one swollen fat leg came to mind. "No—no."

"Well, then. I'd better be seeing who it is." Reece washed his hands and dried them on a towel.

"Follow me to the bar. You'll be able to see her better from there."

"*Her?* Ah—good." His brother's eyes brightened.

"Not so fast. I want Ma to see her too."

"Huh?"

"Come on," Aedan said in a huff.

When he reached his mother standing behind

the bar, she'd already seen the redhead. She motioned with a quick nod in the young woman's direction.

"I know." Aedan smoothed the short hair on his chin as he waited for some sort of verbal response from his family.

Reece strained his neck to see what the commotion was about. His mouth dropped open. He took two steps backward and fell in a seated position. The stool he bumped in the process protested with a thumping noise as it teetered.

"You okay?" Aedan pulled up his brother.

"Aye. What's she doing here?"

"So you do think it's Iona?"

Reece frowned. "Who else could it be?"

"She says she's from the States and her name is Greta Conner."

"Maybe she's Iona reincarnated."

Aedan half laughed. "But wouldn't she have to be dead to be reincarnated?"

"You don't think—" His brother's eyes widened in mock fear.

"I don't." He shook his head at his brother's humor.

"Well, I've heard she's fallen in with a bunch of bad eggs, dodgy to be sure." Reece's eyes darkened.

"I'd have to get a better look." Ma wiped her glasses with a towel. "You know how people can sometimes look alike. If it is Iona, don't worry about it. It's water under the bridge, it is."

"But—" The word came out a bit too loud, and Aedan's heart began to pound.

His mother stopped him with one look.

"It's Iona. Ah, sure look it." Reece glared at the woman who called herself Greta. "What are you going to do?"

"I said I'd give her a glass. So I'll give her a glass." He took in a breath, nodded a fond farewell to his mother and brother, and headed off to his fate.

****

Greta touched the fresh, soft flower and glanced at other occupied tables in the café. A lucky girl must not have gotten the flowers. Each table sported a vase with a single carnation and a jar with a candle.

The tabletops were natural wood, the table legs a purplish color same as the chairs. Didn't look too bad, but it kind of clashed with the peach colored walls. Off to her left, a large mirror in a gold frame was positioned opposite the windows facing the street. She'd like to see the room in the morning. The grand mirror would help reflect daylight in the square room. As it was, several warm colored lights hung from the ceiling.

At the far end stood a bar constructed of dark wood. Behind it were shelves of bottles and kegs. To the right of the bar an open entrance led to the kitchen.

Several families and groups of couples occupied the tables around her. How nice that she wasn't the only one being served a late dinner.

Greta read the placemat which took the place of

a menu while conversations and laughter competed for attention. For breakfast one could choose from a full breakfast or scones, sausage, and eggs. Dinner and lunch had the offering of fish with chips and Irish stew. Varieties of beer took up the biggest section.

A movement by her shoulder caught the corner of her eye. Aedan stood by her table. He probably wanted to know what beer she wanted to drink, since he offered to get her a glass.

"Hello." He smiled. "Glad you stopped in. What can I get for you? How about Beamish? Brewed in Cork since 1792.

She noticed the same New Yorkers from before at a table in the center of the room. The parents each had beer. A youngish couple seated nearest to her also had the same. Greta knew she wouldn't drink it, but didn't want to disappoint him or cause a social rift.

He waited with uplifted eyebrows.

"Yes, thank you. And fish and chips." She inwardly cringed that she'd used the Irish accent on him when they met. At home, it seemed so perfect. "Also a glass of water, please."

He blinked in surprise. What could be so startling about her request? She'd agreed to his offered drink and ordered what everyone else had on their table. *Ugh.*

He nodded. "I'll be right back."

She kept her focus on him. He made his way to the bar where an animated conversation took place. He gestured with his hands as he talked to an older, plump blonde and a cute guy his age with dark hair.

The group looked in her direction and became silent. Each went their own way. The conversation had to be about her. What was the consensus? Did they all think she looked like his ex-girlfriend?

Greta had tried to visualize what it would be like when she arrived in Ireland. She thought the trip would almost be like coming home. She'd dreamed about the place and the people ever since childhood and thought it was one place where she could belong—where she would be accepted. Didn't the Irish love people with red hair? She guessed at least one of them did at one time.

Aedan returned with a tray and gently set the beer, water, and the dinner in front of her. He proceeded to light the candle with a lighter. A flame spurted out then died. He hesitated and glanced at her before giving it another go. After several tries, he finally got the candle lit.

"There you go, Miss Greta. Can I get you anything else?"

"Thank you, no." She attempted a smile. "It looks great. I'm starved."

"Well, enjoy. I'll come back to check on you."

The fish had a nice crusty coating. She didn't see any description of it anywhere other than fish and chips. Knowing what kind and the type of batter it was coated in would be nice. Actually a menu that one could hold instead of an info-placemat would be a lot better. Her background in advertising always found a way to voice its opinion.

After eating one fillet, she took a small sip of beer, trying hard not to wince. The taste made her blink and cringe. She glanced toward the bar to see

Aedan who averted his gaze. He'd seen her look of pain. Oh well, not everyone liked beer. She managed several sips to be polite and surveyed the glass. The gold liquid had gone down about an inch. Good enough.

The young couple at the table next to her finished their meal and paid the clean-shaven man with dark hair like Aedan's. He looked her up and down, even gawked at her shoes, then came and asked if she needed anything. She didn't.

The waiter made his way to the bar and another discussion occurred with many hand gestures on his part. Aedan shook his head a few times, and the blonde lifted her hand, as if emphasizing that she had no idea, or that something was crazy. Aedan tilted his head down and frowned. His fingers smoothed his beard at the jaw line.

Aedan looked in her direction, his eyes met hers. He elbowed the waiter. All three studied her, their faces turning somber. Then, as before, each went their own way.

Greta stifled a sarcastic chuckle. This was what she'd waited twenty two years for? She finished eating the fish and potatoes, not paying attention to where Aedan might be lurking. Instead, she enjoyed the scenery outside on the quiet street.

She needed to find a place to stay and didn't relish the idea of searching for one at night. The hotels she saw before coming to O'Riain's Cottage had charm, but there was something about this pink, four-story building. A room on the top floor, or better yet, a tiny room, would be fun and cozy.

"Can I get you anything else?" Aedan appeared

by her table.

"No, thank you." Greta handed him her empty plate with the silverware resting on it. "The dinner was very good."

He seemed genuinely happy to hear her remark. His eyes brightened and he smiled, then his expression turned serious. "Please don't think it's too forward, but me mother is concerned if you are traveling alone."

Greta kept silent, even though it was obvious that he waited for her answer, whether she was alone, meeting someone, or traveling with a group. She glanced at the bar. The blonde must be his mother. She was in a deep conversation with the waiter who had an uncanny resemblance to Aedan. Had to be his brother. Why hadn't she noticed it before?

"She hates to see a tourist by herself—I mean— the locals here are good people and you are safe enough. It's people passing through that we're unsure of."

A twinge of uneasiness swept through her as a vision of the pasty-skinned murderer revisited.

Chapter 2

Aedan stopped by the front desk. "Did she get a room?"

Ma looked him in the eye and gave no answer.

"Well?" He glanced at the key tags.

"Aye. She went to move her car. You help her with her luggage."

"Why?" It wasn't common for him to drop everything to carry bags and suitcases.

"She requested a small room—the smallest that we have. On the top floor."

"And you gave it to her? We haven't put anyone up there for...for..."

"I know. While she's moving her car, you'd better leg it up there and make sure everything is in order." She handed him the duplicate key. Her usual light-hearted smile had disappeared.

"Ah. Great."

He left the room as quickly as he could without causing alarm. Last thing he wanted was the customers wondering if there was a problem. He hustled up the stairway to the fourth floor.

The floor boards creaked from not being walked on for almost half a year. Hopefully they wouldn't creak quite so bad when their guest arrived. He opened the room, stepped inside, and turned on the lights. The room appeared tidy. Thank goodness. The dresser, night stand, and circular table had a slight covering of dust, which he smoothed off with his shirt sleeves. Good thing he wore a gray shirt. He clicked on the telly, made sure a couple of channels worked, and turned it off.

Next he cracked open the window for some fresh air, plumped the pillows, and gave the quilt on the single, twin-sized bed a good shake then repositioned it.

A quick look in the beige bathroom showed everything was clean and in order, complete with soap and toilet paper.

He turned off all the lights and shut the door while brushing off his shirt sleeves. Taking a running start down the hallway, he practically flew down the steps almost careening into the redhead who called herself Greta. He thought of the saying about keeping your friends close and your enemies closer. Aye, right. The room Ma had given her was directly above his bedroom.

"Oh, hello. I got a room. I go up these stairs?"

Greta motioned with her key, and the maroon tag with the number 408 swung back and forth.

"That's right. Hand over the bags. I'll help you."

She hesitated before handing him a flowered piece of luggage. "Thank you."

"I can take the other one, too." He motioned with his free hand.

Again she hesitated when she gave him an old tweed suitcase. "Thanks. That's awfully nice of you to do that."

"My pleasure." He tried to think of it as a pleasure, so as not to be lying and headed up the stairs with the load. "I have a question for you."

"Okay." Her voice came from behind him.

"When you first spoke to me you had—"

"An Irish accent, I know. I practiced it for a long time, so I could fit in. But…I felt rather foolish not being myself. I'm sorry."

"No apology needed." If only he could come to grips with how Iona had treated him and say the same to her. The young woman, if she wasn't Iona, had to be her twin.

He wouldn't let Iona get away with tricking him. He'd play along, calling her Greta. Then when she turned on him to call him an eejit for not realizing it was her—he could say he knew all along. Maybe he'd find a way to tell her exactly what he thought of her in a sneaky kind of way. If she had any heart at all maybe she'd feel guilty. Aye, right. That would be the day.

Yet, there was something different about her that made him wonder. She appeared wholesome with light makeup. Her clothes were conservative and pretty on her small frame. The lavender sweater complimented her hair and light blue eyes. Her flowered skirt actually came to her knees. What if she truly was Greta Conner? No, couldn't be. He'd go along with the act, well enough that *he* could win some fancy acting award.

"So, you're from Indiana?" He turned to see her response.

"That's right. It's pretty uninteresting—I mean—compared to here. But, funny thing—the state of Indiana is the same size as Ireland."

"Really, now? Just the one little state?"

She nodded and her cheeks turned a darker shade of pink.

"Ah well, here's your room." He waited until she unlocked it, then set her luggage inside the doorway and turned on the light.

She put a hand in her sweater pocket, probably to pull out tip money.

"No—no." He waved. "It was nothing. Good night."

He hustled back through the hallway and down the steps. What was he thinking? He should've taken it. Iona owed him about a hundred euros. Not to mention the other fiasco. But wait, he did the right thing not taking it, perchance—and it was a slim one—that she was Greta. He needed to treat her like she was Greta but keep in mind that she was Iona and help her to come to a feeling of remorse. That wouldn't insult Greta, if she was Greta. He sighed as a wave of fatigue rushed over him. This wasn't going to be easy.

When he was almost all the way down the steps, he nearly ran into his mother.

"How'd it go? Is she all settled? Did she like the room?" His ma held onto the banister to steady herself from the near collision.

"Yes, fine. She didn't say, but she seemed pleased enough." Greta's light blue eyes that sparkled when she smiled came to mind.

"Since I got a better look at her and talked to her, I don't think she's Iona." Ma shook her head.

"Why? Because of her American accent?"

"That and something else I can't put a finger on, but—"

"Remember what I said earlier? She had plans of going to America to study to be an actress. It'd be just like her to—"

"To do what, exactly?"

"She's out to make me look the biggest fool ever. Wouldn't it be like her to pretend to be someone else, make me fall for her all over again, just to dump me?"

"I don't know. Isn't that awfully petty?"

A weighted sigh escaped as he slowly closed and opened his eyes. His forehead felt like a mass of wrinkles. "We're talking Iona here."

"Oh, right. Well, maybe. She was a one to thrive on discord and trouble. A jealous sort, too. What did you see in her?"

"That's a good question." He took a step toward the dining room as a way of ending the conversation. The answer wasn't something to say to one's mother.

"Because she's a hot little minx." She bobbed

her head.

"Oh, Ma." He rolled his eyes.

"Blimey. I'm older *and* your mother, but I'm not blind. I was young once ye know."

"Uh, huh." *Oh bother.* He took another step, but she stopped him.

"What about her ID? It had her picture and name, Greta—"

He waved a hand to dismiss the thought. "Those can be forged."

"Oh, I be a doubting it."

Aedan shook his head. Ma was always good at having the last word.

****

Greta took in the surroundings of the room about the same dimensions as her walk-in closet at home. The tan wall behind the twin bed had no decorations, and the other three walls were covered in some sort of paneling or perhaps it was the actual wall. She walked to the window, the floor creaking with each step. The street below was quiet, not a soul in sight. Beside her, a TV perched on a dresser. She smiled. Aedan's mother had told her that she'd have piped telly in her room. Somehow piped telly sounded better than cable TV.

Greta sat on the bed that promptly creaked. The bedcover was a handmade quilt in shades of tan, yellow, and cream. The material had been cut in squares and sewn together. Could be that someone in Aedan's family had made it. She slipped her phone out of her purse and laid back, putting her head on the pillow. The back of her head sunk way in and the white pillow bunched up around her cheeks, almost knocking the phone out of her hand.

"Hi, Dad, I made it." She returned to a sitting position, listening to a voice she could barely hear. "Uh-huh. Yeah, no problems."

Her luggage sat against the wall in her line of vision. How sweet of Aedan to offer to carry it for her. His smile and blue-gray eyes were so kind, welcoming her—a stranger. True she was just a customer. But not everyone looked like his ex-girlfriend. He had to have bad feelings toward his ex, yet treated her like she was someone special.

"I'm sorry, what?" She didn't want to admit that she'd zoned out for a second.

The phone connection wavered in and out. It didn't really matter though. He was only being nice and going through the motions. Why hadn't he told her sooner that he wasn't her biological father? Her heart pounded. She'd needed her birth certificate to get her passport, and it was the first time she read through it. Other times, her dad held onto the document. Why was it so important to keep it secret? But now that she knew, things seemed different and strained.

"Yes, it's beautiful. I love it here. Well, I have to go. I'll keep in touch through email."

Another quiet response sounded in her ear that she didn't have to guess at.

"Yes, love you, too. Bye."

Her father did love her; she had to give him that.

Her eyes blurred with tears. He'd treated her just like she was his own. She'd tried to talk to him about it before she boarded the plane, but his new girlfriend, Joanie, always caused drama. She tried to push the scene out of her mind, but it played again like a bad dream.

"Dad, about the birth certificate—"

"You put it back safely in the file?" He always worried about misplacing things.

"Yes, but the name—" Greta stiffened to see Joanie put an arm around her dad's waist as a big drop of frosting from her cupcake landed on her sweater.

"Don't worry dear, the names are correct." He handed Joanie a tissue from his pocket.

"What?" Upset surged within Greta. How could he be so blasé and abrupt? "Can you at least tell me—"

A voice on the loud speaker interrupted her. She had to board her flight. She'd clenched her jaw determined to find the answers on her own.

****

Aedan turned off the kitchen lights. Everything was clean and ready for tomorrow. Reece gave him a weak salute and shuffled ahead of him to the third floor where the family apartment was located.

"You know, it sure would be nice to have a life," Reece said as he disappeared into his room.

"It would." Aedan didn't have any reserve

energy to expound on the subject. Lately, it had been his way of saying goodnight. They'd talked of it too many times to count and, besides that, Reece had already shut his door.

"Goodnight." His mother switched off the family room light.

"Goodnight." He called into the darkness, stepped into his room, and shut the door.

He'd just slipped out of his clothes and into his flannel pants, when a knock sounded at his door. His brother must still want to commiserate.

"Reece, I'm way too tired—oh. Ma, what is it?"

"Thank you for working so hard today. I do appreciate it." Her voice waivered with emotion.

"It's okay. Don't worry. Things will get better." He hoped to comfort her.

"Right now it's a strain on all of us. Well...get some good sleep."

"I will." He softly closed the door.

He climbed into bed feeling an emotional weight along with being physically tired. The days were so long. He sought to find some solution to the problem as he had many times before. The three of them were barely making it. They had just enough money to buy fresh fish tomorrow. The income from the Iona/Greta girl staying a week would help. Even so, financial collapse seemed right around the corner. There had to be some way to make things better. Get more business—get a life.

He couldn't make his eyes stay open or keep his thoughts on track, when a creak sounded overhead. He prayed Greta would sleep soundly. The noise sounded again as she must have turned in bed. Not that it was a loud sound, but it irritated him like dripping water.

Another knock sounded at the door. "Ah. Great." Ma probably had something else to say. He hoped she wasn't crying.

He opened the door. "What, Ma—oh. Reece. What is it?"

"Are you going after the redhead? If you don't, I will. Fair warning, okay?"

"You're codding. The wee doll said she'd only be here a week."

"Ah, brother. Don't you know your whole life can change in a week?"

****

Next morning, Aedan wished he could've called in sick, but there he was helping prepare breakfast. At intervals all through the night, the bed a floor above him creaked as the sleepless owner tossed and turned.

"You don't look so good. What did you do? Sneak out and have some fun?" Reece cracked eggs and plopped them in a pan.

"Aye, right." Aedan gripped a knife and sliced through an onion.

"Well, that onion spray ought to help your bloodshot eyes." Reece snickered. "Oh, there goes your lady-love."

"What?" He focused on the dining room and front door. Sure enough, out went Greta. He noted that she wasn't walking very fast. Even from a good distance, she looked pale and tired. She must be as bad off as he was.

"Guess that's one less person for breakfast." Reece picked up a mushroom and scrutinized it.

"I'm going to need more coffee."

"Wonder where she's going? At least you know she'll be coming back here sooner or later, aye?" His brother poked him with his elbow. "Iona sure can pull off the good-girl look. Letting her hair go natural and growing it longer made quite a good change."

"I'm going to need more coffee."

Reece scratched his head. "You already said that."

"She has changed some, but I know it's her."

"It's the dental work that really makes her look different."

"That's the only thing that threw me off. But you're right. Having her teeth straightened and whitened makes a big difference." Aedan finished dicing the onion.

"Plus, she's filled out a little more—a little more curvy."

"Eh?" Aedan didn't like his brother's tone, but he agreed with a nod.

"If you're not going after her, I will." Reece glanced at him with a sly grin.

"We're not on that again?"Aedan slammed down the knife on the cutting board. "You'll do no such thing. Isn't it enough what she did to me? You really want that kind of trouble? That kind of heartache?"

Reece shrugged a shoulder. "She's changed. She's not the same."

"It's an act. That's what she wants us to believe. You'll not go after her." He felt his eyes bugging out as he pointed at his brother. "She's out to banjax us."

"I'm not so sure."

"No. Reece, no." He shook his head as his brother continued to grin.

Fuming over Reece's remarks was the only thing that kept him going the rest of the day. He didn't like how his brother kept an eye out for Greta. Aedan not only had to watch out for her return, he had to watch out for his sneaky brother, too.

Finally at the evening meal, Greta strolled in and sat at the same table as the night before. Reece made a move to step in front of him and elbow him out of the way, but Aedan shot forward, grabbed a pad of paper and a pen, and practically speed-walked to her table.

"Hello there, Miss Greta. I missed you." Then he realized what his dumb tongue said. He didn't mean to say that. "How are you? Have a nice day?"

"Yes. Fine." She blinked and kept her eyes focused on her placemat for a few long seconds before glancing up at him. "How are you?"

"Exhausted. It's been quite a day."

"I'm really tired, too."

He nodded, knowing the reason. It was all that tossing and turning. "What can I get for you?"

She studied the placemat with a sad expression. "What I'd really like is the breakfast that I missed.

It smelled so good."

"Okay. What would you like to drink?"

"What? You mean I can have breakfa—"

"We serve it all day."

"I didn't know—couldn't tell. Tea. I'll have hot tea with milk."

He wrote down her order even though it was ingrained in his mind. "We'll have it served up in just a few." *Wrong*. Didn't she know that American's don't order tea with milk? Although, she'd managed to speak with the American accent pretty well.

He turned to leave then stepped back. "Sugar too?"

She nodded.

Of course.

Aedan handed over the order to Reece without a word. His brother looked it over and nodded with a raised eyebrow.

"When the eggs are done, I'll take the plate to her. I'm going to ask her to join me for coffee tonight." Reece grabbed a pan.

Aedan's heart skipped a beat. "No...no, you can't." Besides being a bad idea, she'd never sleep with all the caffeine.

"Why?" Reece taunted and poked his chest. "You aren't going to."

"I am." Aedan tried his best to glare at his brother. "So I'll take her the plate, thank you."

Reece's eyes widened and his eyebrows shot up. He turned away from Aedan and cleared his throat. His brother had to be hiding laughter. Was the whole thing a joke to him?

****

Greta looked forward to the plate of breakfast food coming, although she wasn't exactly sure what she'd be getting. The placemat had a list, but she didn't want everything. Hopefully Aedan would bring her what she saw this morning which was more of an omelet. Funny though, omelets weren't on the menu.

Aedan came out with a tray and served steak and potatoes to a couple sitting nearby. *No way.* That wasn't on the menu. Maybe she'd been too quick ordering breakfast. She was about to fold the paper mat into a giant airplane when he set her tea in front of her, along with a metal container of milk and a bowl of sugar.

His hand shook a bit, and he almost spilled the tea. What on earth could he be nervous about? Why didn't anything make sense? Maybe she was more tired than she realized.

"Thank you." She smiled and nodded.

He nodded in return, and stepped away.

She plopped two spoonfuls of sugar in her tea, stirred, and poured in milk until it turned a light caramel color. Feeling that someone stared at her, she looked up to see that Aedan hadn't moved very far away and must have watched her prepare her tea.

"I'll be right back with your dinner," he said, and headed toward the kitchen.

While Greta waited, she opened the shopping bag she brought in with her and studied the map she'd purchased. Where was she to go first? She read the names of the cities. Nothing in particular stood out to her, except the village she was in, Angel's Hollow.

Next she pulled out the postcards and sighed. It was like breathing in a breath of fresh air. Several cards pictured a beautiful countryside with castles. But the ones with steep rocky shorelines enthralled her. She'd never grow tired of the view. In her imagination she could even hear the waves crashing against the rocks.

She slipped the map and cards back into the bag and was about to pull out the glass she bought, when Aedan reappeared with a tray.

"Have fun shopping today?" He set an omelet made with fresh vegetables in front of her that made her mouth water.

"Yes." She showed him the *Kiss me, I'm Irish* glass decorated with a leprechaun.

"Nice."

"I also went for a drive and ended up at a park."

"Please, take me with you next time?"

His expression turned serious when his glance reached her face. Did she look worried? She had no idea and smiled, wondering if she appeared nervous.

"Just codding. I hardly ever get out of here." He waved his words away. "Well, enjoy."

He took a step to leave, but then turned back. "Later this evening…would you like to join me for some afters?"

Chapter 3

Aedan straightened up the last few pans and put the two slices of chocolate-orange cake back into the refrigerator. He checked his watch. She was thirty minutes past their meeting time. He had to face it by now that she wasn't coming.

Footsteps in the kitchen startled him.

"What are you doing here?" Aedan couldn't believe his eyes.

"Just wanted to see if I could serve coffee to the love birds." Reece looked into the dining room. "Where is she?"

"Not here. Like old times, right?"

"Don't get yourself all down." His brother patted him on the shoulder. "Does this mean I have a chance after all?"

"No—no, it doesn't."

"Hello, sorry that I'm late." Greta entered the dining room and smoothed her hair.

Aedan gave his brother a shove. "Well, off you go."

"Good night, Miss." Reece gave her a dazzling smile as he passed her.

"You're not too late. What would you like to drink?" Aedan's mind whirled. Did Greta hear their conversation? How much?

"Tea would be nice." She sat at a booth nearest the kitchen and folded her hands.

"Chocolate cake?" he asked, knowing it was one of Iona's favorites.

"I'd never turn down chocolate cake."

Ah ha. He brought the tea and two plates of dessert to the table and sat opposite of her. The only light source came from the kitchen, since technically everything was closed for the night. The dining room seemed too dark, so he lit the candle at the table and then methodically began to add milk and sugar to the tea.

"There you are." He handed her the cup and saucer and prepared his own. "Well, dig in." He motioned to the cake.

"Thank you." She took a bite. "It's wonderful. I like the orange frosting."

"Yes. Nothing like the combination." He forced a smile. "Tell me...tell me about your day."

"Um...where should I start? The shopping? The park?"

"Start at the beginning. From when you left here

this morning. Make it a long story with lots of descriptions." He tried to keep his eyes open and hoped he wouldn't end up face down in the frosting. "I'm so sleepy. It will be like a bedtime story, then I'll shuffle off."

"I went for a walk around town and..." She took a sip of tea. "I saw a man sitting on a bench. He was well-dressed—suit and a hat—had an umbrella, and he was feeding some sort of animal."

"What was it?"

"I don't know." She shook her head. "It kind of looked like a fox with a cat's tail."

"Was it was brown? Have a longish body?"

"Yes."

"Had to be a pine marten."

Her expression sparked like she'd never heard of it before. "Huh?"

"It's a wild animal, something like a weasel. A long time ago, monks used their fur to make brushes to do calligraphy and art work."

"You mean like the *Book of Kells*? I love that."

"Exactly."

"I'm so glad I got to see...a pine marten. It was cute little thing. The man was feeding it bread or something."

"They do like bread with peanut butter."

"So it's a common thing?"

"It does happen occasionally. I mean, not every household has an outdoor pet pine marten." He chuckled then took a bite of cake and waited for her to continue.

"After that, I went shopping. Such a balanced group of shops. I think I could've found a gift for everyone in my family."

"Oh?" What kind of story would she make up about her family?

"Well, not that my family is big."

"Who's the glass for?"

"My brother, but I might keep it for myself."

"What does your brother do?" He took a drink of tea. Had to be an imaginary job, since it was an imaginary brother.

"He's worked a variety of jobs to build up his resume."

"Like what?"

"Service type jobs."

He nodded. "That's good." How much more vague could she be?

"It's kind of a sore spot to him. Dad wanted him to be a doctor." She broke off a small piece of cake. The fork hovered mid-air. "My father is a doctor." She looked down to her plate and set her fork down. The cake still filled its silver prongs.

"I'm sorry if I seem to be prying. I'm not. Just curious—what do you do back in the States? Are you a student? Or—"

"I work at a business firm."

"That must be interesting. What sort?"

"Yes...advertising...but it's nice to take a break."

He coughed and accidentally sputtered. "Really?"

How did she come up with that?

****

Greta opened the door to her room, feeling uplifted. She never thought she could have such a strong connection to a man from a different country. Aedan showed genuine interest in her and her family, and even what she'd experienced throughout the day. She'd told him everything up to the point of falling asleep and not hearing her alarm—the reason she was late.

She guessed falling for an Irishman wasn't so uncommon though, after all, that's what happened to her mother. Well, actually two men. One that was her biological father and the other she'd married.

Even though Aedan was sleepy, he'd paid close attention to her answers. The thoughtful way that he'd mulled them over with his chin supported by his hand and his index finger resting on his sideburn was her undoing.

"So handsome." She hated that she'd said it out loud and looked around the bedroom to see something that she could've been talking to. Nothing. Maybe she's the one who needed a pet pine marten.

She slipped out of her clothes and into a long oversized t-shirt that doubled as a sleep shirt and climbed into the creaky bed. She half expected a spring or two to poke her.

As she was drifting off to sleep, two male voices reached her ears. The tones sounded normal enough, then escalated into arguing. She lifted her head off the pillow to hear more clearly.

"Reece, what do you expect me to do? Fist fight you, for her? I have to go to bed." Aedan's voice sounded distraught. A door clicked shut, then silence.

What could that possibly mean? Aedan had to fight off a girl that was bothering his brother? That couldn't be. Reece looked pretty capable himself. Plus he wouldn't fight a girl. Wait. The words were *fist fight you*. Aedan had to fight his brother? She should've known that Aedan had a girlfriend.

Whatever relationship he had, it didn't seem happy. Somehow his brother was involved. Could be the girl liked Reece more. She sank back into her pillow. Hopefully that was the case.

More muffled voices sounded. This time a woman and a man. Aedan? Determined not to pay attention, she covered her ears with the pillow.

She rolled to her side to get more comfortable. The woman's voice became higher, and then she started to cry. The sound was one of deep trouble and sorrow.

Greta heaved a sigh and tossed the pillow away. The voices were faint, but she could make out the words in the stillness of the night.

"…to me. Ma, it's fine. Things will either start to get better, or we'll figure something out." Aedan's voice.

"It's not good. We need to hire more help, but we can't afford it."

"We're in a tricky spot right now, but things will work out. We'll get more business, and then we can afford to hire more help. Reece and I are okay."

"You're not okay. Don't you think I have eyes in my head?"

"Just give Liam another week or two, and he'll be able to work more. That will help, now won't it?"

"It will. But can you last until then?"

"You know we can. Please don't worry and get off to bed."

"I'll go. I'll go. And I'll pray for a miracle." She blew her nose.

Chapter 4

Next morning, Greta hurried out of O'Riain's Cottage. She caught Aedan's glance and waved at him as she jogged out the door. He'd started to smile and wave back, but she was already outside.

After she took pictures of O'Riain's Cottage and neighboring shops, she set out on a brisk walk to see the pine marten. The sun beat down the freshly wet pavement from a morning rain.

If Aedan could come with her on one of her sightseeing trips, it would be a win-win. She'd get the pleasure of his company, and he'd get away for a while. The thought of him being stuck at work six days out of the week from morning until night made her heart ache. Last night, his eyes had become wistful as she described the park she'd seen. He knew the name of it right away but said he'd never been there. It seemed almost tragic, then again, there were many sights in her hometown and state she'd never seen. But only because she didn't care to see them.

Aedan had bigger worries than seeing a park.

Greta set to work, brainstorming anything that might help the O'Riains. She hated to see any business struggle. Lack of customers usually had to do with poor advertising and in some cases no advertising. Good grief. They didn't even have a decent menu.

One task she wanted to complete on her trip was to find someone to help in honor of her mother. What better tribute to give her mom than to bless someone in Ireland—and it had to be the O'Riain family. They needed advertising, and that was her forte.

She'd walked by the last shop when she realized she hadn't been keeping close track of her surroundings. A glance over her shoulder told her she was too late. Three scruffy guys followed her closely. She swallowed any fear she had, knowing they could sense it on her about as well as a dog.

One of the men spoke up. "You're a fine thing. Could you give us the time?"

She gulped, trying to remember if *give us the time* stood for something else. She turned and looked each of them in the eye. Usually she was a good judge of character, but she couldn't pick up on any vibe, either good or bad. None of them had pasty skin.

Glancing at her watch, she said, "It's five minutes after nine."

For an answer the young, disheveled men gave a series of grunts.

The trio crossed the street. She continued on, seeing the older man on the bench. He wore the same suit and hat. Something moved through the grass near his leg. It had to be the pine marten. She tried to get a good look at the man's character in his face without him noticing. A few steps closer and he'd look up. He reminded her of Indiana Jones's father from the movie *Raiders of the Lost Ark*.

He turned in her direction and looked beyond her. She stiffened and glanced over her shoulder.

"Hey, there." The three guys had returned, getting closer with each second. The short stocky one spoke. "Have any spare coins?"

"My, my, you *are* a fine thing aren't you?" The tallest guy with a black front tooth and a wrinkled jacket stepped out in front of his buddies to be in the lead.

"Got a zonk or two for us?" The dark haired guy in black with a chain around his neck winked at her. Or did he wink? He rubbed his eye.

"You bealin' langers get out of here and leave the miss alone." The voice came from the man on the bench. Except he wasn't sitting anymore.

"Just lookin' for some coins." The guy in black tried to explain and stepped back. He motioned to the other two to turn around and leave.

"Yeah. Well. Get a job." The older man yelled at the three then turned to her. "Sorry that they bothered you. Just kids passing through."

"Thanks…I, uh…thanks." Greta shivered and rubbed her arms. "So glad you were here."

He frowned and nodded.

She glanced around the bench. "Did the pine marten run away?

"If he did, he'll be back." He held a small piece of a peanut butter sandwich.

"I was hoping to get a picture of him. He's so cute." Greta pulled her camera out of her purse.

"He should come—there he is—little dickens."

She clicked a picture as the animal took the food from the man's hand. "I'm Greta, by the way."

The man nodded.

"Does he have a name?" She pointed at the pine marten.

"He does. You heard it."

"Dickens?"

"Aye." He chuckled. "And the first name of Charles."

"Aw. Cute." She wanted to tease him by asking if the little animal wrote tales, but smiled instead."

His eyes squinted in the sunlight as he gazed at her face. "Sure look like you're from Eire, but you're not…are you?"

****

Greta stepped into the nearby library, thankful that she'd asked for directions in one of the shops. Otherwise she might have driven far out of her way, not knowing the old brick building housed a library.

Ivy covered the side facing the small parking lot and nearly covered the sign.

A cheerful girl behind the counter exchanged smiles with Greta as she headed to several tables where young people had their laptops hooked up to the internet.

She pulled her laptop out of her bag, attached the cord to the connection in the table, and then grabbed a paper from her purse. Her biological father's name was Padraig O'Cnaimhin. Her hands perspired as she typed the name into a phonebook search for Ireland. Matches popped up. A few just had the initial P for the first name. It was a place to start. She copied the information.

Next she sent an email to Dad letting him know that everything was fine, and it might be days before she could write again.

With those tasks out of the way, she relaxed and checked the photos she'd transferred from her camera. The shot of O'Riain's Cottage showed the pink building contrasting with the deep blue sky. The bright flowers in the planters, and the brick sidewalk added to the charm. Next was a colorful group of shops: red store—pottery; dark green building—fine linens; yellow—cut crystal; and the cute, light-pink bakery with an array of pastel sprinkles painted on the building.

She clicked on the travel sites and blogs that she'd perused before coming to Ireland. On each site, she signed on and wrote a little blurb about O'Riain's Cottage, mentioning their rustic rooms, hearty Irish cuisine, and great location to shops within walking distance. Then she uploaded the photos. That should help. Sightseers always welcomed tips from fellow travelers.

Gritting her teeth, she googled O'Riain's Cottage. Nothing came up, thank goodness. Last thing she wanted to see was a poorly designed website. Greta could start on it soon, if the family approved. Then they needed several strategically placed ads with the web address. Maybe more than several.

The menu required immediate attention. Plus an outdoor sign to tempt passers-by, stating the special of the day. They'd also need postcards and business cards.

How could she give Aedan all her ideas without alienating or overwhelming him? And would he even trust her? He'd think she was being nice in order to sell him advertising. Not her goal at all. She wanted to do it free of charge, anonymously. But how could she pull it off?

She'd have to think on that. First off—a good menu design...and a look-see at the competition.

****

Aedan observed Reece smoothing fresh herbs over two pork roasts. His brother loved to try new things. "Preparing food is definitely your talent. I'll give you that much."

"It is. And how much better it would be if we had enough customers to put all this meat away." Reece covered the pan and slid it in the oven. "How about a nice salad to go with it?"

Aedan nodded. "If you want to take some of the extra to old Mrs. McFeely, I'll cover for you. She'd love it."

"Ah. Well. I'd better make some bubble and squeak then. She's fond of English fry-ups."

"Don't forget to add another dinner for her cranky next door neighbor, Mrs. Donovan."

Reece chuckled. "Aye, right. But I think you should take it to them. It'd be a few minutes away from here—a good break."

Maybe his brother was right. "Well, I..." Aedan caught Reece's expression. That conniving grin again. What was he up to now? "Oh, I see."

"What?" His face turned innocent.

"You want me out of the way, so you can make a move when Greta comes back."

"Really? Brother? Am I *that* easy to read?" Reece balanced a cabbage on his fingertips. "No—no. You're wrong."

"What is it then?"

"You *need* a break."

Not if it meant missing Greta and letting her fall into Reece's devices. Or rather him falling into Greta's devices. One thing he knew; they both had devices.

"If you happen not to be here when Greta comes, I'll be sure to talk to her and—"

"Reece. Watch yourself."

"Invite her to go to church with us tomorrow morning."

****

After sending out a few more emails to her friends and coworkers, Greta set out to taste-test the other restaurants in town.

Starting with a full breakfast at the first café probably wasn't the best idea. At lunch time, she tried two different places, eating only half and taking the rest with her. When she got back in her car and saw the amount of food, she realized she'd never have the opportunity to eat it. She wanted to try out a different place at dinner.

She drove by the older man's bench. He still sat there. Without giving it any thought, she stopped and got out of the car with the bags.

"Hi. Me again," she said.

The man's glance went from the white bags to her face. "Charles Dickens went back to his home."

"That's okay." She sat on the bench beside him. "I needed to do some research on a couple of the restaurants here—"

"Hmm?"

"And I couldn't eat all of the lunches. Would you help me out? I'd hate for it to go to waste."

"Did you like it?" He smoothed his hat.

She nodded and held the bags toward him.

"Well, then. I'd be happy to help you out." He took hold of the bags with rough-looking hands.

"Thanks. And thank you for helping me earlier."

"You're welcome." His eyes twinkled, and he tipped his hat.

"I hope I'll see you and Charles tomorrow." She stood to leave.

"Me too." He waved.

Before she drove away, his image appeared in

the side mirror. He'd opened one of the bags and had taken a big bite out of one of the sandwiches.

Greta jotted down notes on the restaurants, including her feelings on the atmosphere, waitresses' attitudes, prices, selection, and quality. She meandered through several shops and experienced an outdoor market until dinner time arrived. She chose a busy eatin' house as the locals called them.

She stepped into O'Sullivan's green building through a heavy wooden door and waited with a couple of groups. The dark teal walls were decorated in a nautical type theme. The aroma of fried fish and chips filled the air. Restaurant noises of people talking and clattering silverware became louder as the hostess guided her though a hallway into the dining room.

Seated at a brown lacquered table, she looked over the menu and her surroundings. A handsome man with blond hair wielding an acoustic guitar stepped to a wooden stool and pulled a microphone stand closer. His mellow voice filled the restaurant. The folk music charmed her, and patrons began to clap. Still amidst all the commotion, a certain man with dark hair and a beard occupied her thoughts.

By the time Greta left, she could hardly breathe from eating too much. As she made her way to the car, she consoled herself. The dinner salad in her stomach would shrink down soon, plus she had a better idea what the O'Riains were up against.

****

"You can run off now on your errand." The direction of Ma's eyes pointed to the door.

"What errand?" Aedan could guess, but he wanted to hear it from her lips.

"Take old Mrs. McFeely her dinner. Reece told me." She shooed him along. "Such a great idea, we should do it more often. We've neglected her too long."

"I thought Reece was going to deliver it."

"He's got it all packaged up—here it is." She handed him the bags from under the bar. "Reece can't take it. He's tending several things on the cooker."

"Of course he is."

"Off you go. Mind you, the other bag is for her cranky neighbor. He phoned them to let them know you're coming."

Ah...great. But maybe Reece's plan would backfire. Hopefully he'd be busy with whatever he had on the cook-stove when Greta returned.

"Don't worry, Liam and I will take good care of the customers." His mother gave him a tap on the shoulder.

"Aye, but Liam's getting ready to leave." Aedan passed by a smirking Reece then stepped out the backdoor.

If he had to do it, then haste had to be the way to go. The shortest time he was gone, the better. He slid into the red Volkswagen Jetta and placed the bagged dinners on the passenger seat. He gripped the wheel. Why was he stressing so? What could be the worst that would happen?

Aedan kept his eyes on the road as his mind

wandered. The worst, of course, would be Reece marrying Iona. At first she'd keep the happy love thing going, and then she'd micromanage his life. Suddenly Reece would have to give up his restaurant dream and work for her father in the peat field while she had a string of affairs, using whatever money he brought home. Reece would eventually find out, if he didn't get murdered first by one of Iona's jealous lovers. There'd be a divorce, and O'Riain's Cottage would have to be sold because she'd want her half. Then they'd be left with nothing….

His pulse quickened. Plus if they had any kids, the poor, sweet darlings would be brought up by a wench. With her filthy language and men running in and out. She and the children would end up getting murdered because of all the money she owed questionable characters.

No. He couldn't let that happen. The only thing in the future forecast was death and destruction. Aedan's fingers began to hurt. His vice-like grip on the wheel was so tight; it took an effort to get his hand to move. "Ah—Reece. You have to be smarter than *that*."

Still fuming with his head pounding, he pulled up to Mrs. McFeely's home. The wee, white-haired woman stood by her open door. Next house over on the right, Mrs. Donovan waited with a big frown and bleary eyes.

Aedan stepped out of his car and waved. "Hello. I have your dinners."

"Bless you, dear." Mrs. McFeely clasped her hands and gave a little hop.

He walked toward her house and up the few steps. "Here you go. I hope you enjoy it."

"Thank you." She took the package and her eyes gleamed. "Did you bring a dinner for Mrs. Donovan?"

"I have it right here." He glanced over to Mrs. Donovan's direction. The woman with plastered down gray hair still frowned as she stared back. He jogged down the steps. "Bye, now. Take care."

Mrs. McFeely smiled, waved, and closed the door. The door shot open. "I will see you in church tomorrow?"

"To be sure." He nodded as she smiled and the door closed once more.

He hurried to Mrs. Donovan's house. "Here you go, Mrs. Donovan. Hope you enjoy—"

The older lady took the package, heaved a heavy sigh, and shut the door.

Ah, well. Worse things could happen.

As he opened the car door, Mrs. McFeely's front door opened again and her small voice sang out. "Reece, could you help with me microwave? It's such a pretty dinner, and I'd hate to eat it cold."

"Okay. But I'm not Reece."

"What now?"

"I'm Aedan."

"Aedan? You handsome fellas all look alike."

****

Greta sat at her table in the dining room at O'Riain's. Even though the paper placemat was fresh, it didn't incite any interest. Scanning the room, she sadly noted that the walls didn't have anything to look at either. On the plus side, the red carnation on the table still looked perky.

A movement caught her eye. Aedan's mother started toward her with a pad of paper and a pen. Greta hoped she'd understand that she only wanted something to drink. Before she could make it to her table, Aedan's brother appeared. He looked revved up or surprised with a slight smile on his face. He waved his paper and pen at his mother. She rolled her eyes and held up a hand. Her jaw went slack with a scoff.

"Hello there." He smiled. "I don't think we've officially met. I'm Reece." He turned to look to the middle of the room. "It's okay, Ma. I've got it."

"I know. I'm not blind." His mother headed back toward the bar.

"Well now, what can I get for you? The special?"

Greta studied the placemat. "On here?"

"It's not listed on there. Today's special is a lovely pork roast seasoned with garlic, rosemary, and thyme. It comes with a salad of fresh greens, tomatoes, parmesan cheese, and a light, house dressing. Also included is a side-order of bubble and squeak." His voice flowed, almost with a poetic quality.

"I'll take it." She smiled. "And I don't even know what bubble and squeak is."

"It's an English fry-up of cabbage and

potatoes."

"Awesome. But please, could you make the portions small. I mean very, very small."

"I'll see what I can do. And what to drink?"

With all the food and overeating, she needed something fizzy. "A Diet Coke."

"Very good." Reece turned on his heel.

No, it was very stupid. How much farther could her stomach stretch? She couldn't resist his charm. Why-oh-why? If his mother would've taken her order, she'd have only ordered a drink.

Greta shot a look at his retreating back. She'd wanted to ask him a question, but it was too late. Reece stepped into the kitchen and disappeared from view. More importantly, where was Aedan? Maybe he'd rounded up a little time off to see his girlfriend.

She looked out the window. The rays from the setting sun glowed on the shop across the street. A smiling couple walked by, each holding their child's hand. They swung him back and forth as they moved along. Even from inside the restaurant she could hear his squeal of joy. Aw, if only she could find the love of her life and have a family. Sometimes it seemed everyone around her paired off, leaving her the single one out. Even if she remained single, she'd determined long ago that she trusted God with her life.

"Here you are." Reece set her drink and dinner in front of her. The enticing aroma tempted her, even though she had no room left. "Do the portions look right? I can bring you more."

"It's perfect. Thank you."

He nodded and took a step to leave.

"Oh, I wanted to ask you a question."

"Sure, what is it?"

"The other times I ordered from the menu." She touched the placemat. "I didn't know you had specials. Do you have specials every day?"

Reece's blue-gray eyes studied her face so intently that she began to feel warm. "Aedan took your order each time, right?"

"Yes." Greta inwardly sighed. She didn't want to get him into any trouble.

Reece sat in the chair opposite her as he muttered. "Oh, my, my, my." He rubbed his chin with an index finger. "Usually, Aedan is so good at explaining the specials…it had to be because…"

She waited. It had to be her likeness to his ex-girlfriend that threw him off.

"You look like Iona." His gaze locked onto her eyes and seemed to study every minute expression. He almost seemed accusatory.

"I…his ex-girlfriend." She swallowed.

"One look at you and the specials must've flown from his mind."

Greta felt compelled to apologize but kept her mouth closed.

"She's hurt him on several different levels—broke his heart, took his money, ran his good name through the dirt." His brow furrowed. "Aye, he fell for her really hard. I hope he can come to a point of forgiving her and forgetting…for his own sake."

"I'm sorry to hear that." She twisted the napkin in her lap.

"Ah. Don't worry about it. You're a sweet dear.

I've said way too much. But next time…" he smiled as he leaned toward her, "ask about the specials."

She smiled in return. How could she not with his cute face so close to hers? "Okay."

"Need anything else?" His glance shifted to the table.

"No, I'm fine, thanks." *Ugh.*

Reece stood and walked away.

Greta's stomach churned. He'd made her feel like she was Iona. Why heave grief and accusation on an innocent customer?

Oh, no. If Reece held all that negativity toward Iona, Aedan's had to be much worse. He only saw Iona when he looked at her. The bad memories best forgotten were being brought to the forefront of his mind. Greta's whole involvement here was a mistake.

She took a bite of the pork roast. Tender, juicy, delicious. The single best thing that she'd had since being in Angel's Hollow. The salad offered a crunch of freshness with a light zingy taste. And the bubble and squeak was hearty and tasty.

The O'Riains had a lot going for them and their customers were probably due to word of mouth. Not bad. That's how Aedan got her here by offering her a glass. Why did she have to get stuck in all this? Being kind to her must be like facing dragons and charging them head on.

****

Aedan pulled into a parking spot and shot through the back door. Reece stirred a pot on the cooker, looked over his shoulder, and wiggled his eyebrows at him.

"What's that supposed to mean?" Aedan washed his hands at the sink.

"It means, dear brother, that we have fresh hot fudge sauce for the ice cream in the freezer. I'm going to ask the *American woman* to join me for afters."

"She's here—she's out there?"

"Aye, just about done eating too."

Aedan took a deep breath and stepped out into the dining area. Apparently Greta had finished eating, paid Ma, and was standing to leave. She picked up a notebook and a few packages that she had beside her. She slipped a paper placemat into one of the bags.

She looked in his direction, blushed an encompassing color of dark pink that covered her whole face, and waved with a few free fingers. He blinked and held up a hand to wave, but she'd turned away and headed toward the stairs.

He hurried through the room. When he reached the stairs, she was nowhere in sight. She could hustle up those stairs as quick as he could. At least it meant that Reece didn't have the opportunity to ask her to have dessert. But did he talk to her or ask her anything else? His shoulders sagged. Reece had to have talked to her. Whatever he'd said made her blush when she saw him. Not good. Not good at all. Now things would be really strange, as if they weren't before.

****

Greta placed the notebook and bags on the round table in her room. She'd been enthused about her purchases and ideas, but now? She didn't even bother to take them out of the bag. Feeling like an overfilled balloon, she clicked on the television and sat on the bed. What looked to be a British mystery movie popped up on the screen. Perfect. She needed to forget everything for a while and rethink it later. Her eyelids became heavy and the bed more comfortable.

Sometime later, she opened her eyes to a darkened room, TV still playing. She turned off the movie, plunging the room into complete darkness except for the faint street light from the window. Determined to go back to sleep, she kicked off her shoes, got back in bed, and covered up. The poor bed acted like it was getting killed from the way it creaked.

Finally she settled in a comfortable position, not easy considering she still wore her jeans and button-up shirt. Her eyes sprung open, and she forced them closed.

****

Aedan listened to muffled screams and gun shots, coming from the telly on the floor above his room. Hopefully the detective would catch the bad guy soon and have it over and done with. Aedan wrestled his pillow over his head to help block out the sounds. Ah, silence. But it became too silent. He lifted the pillow, fearing he'd gone deaf. Greta had turned the telly off. Thank goodness.

He turned over and checked the clock. Two thirty. No way. He wouldn't be able to function, but at least it was Sunday. He'd go to church then come home and crash.

A noise made him open his eyes. Oh, no. Another creaking session as she tossed and turned. Had she been asleep during the movies, and now she was awake for the day?

Perhaps this was how she meant to finish the job and drive him mad.

Reece's idea of inviting her to church wasn't a bad one. Maybe Iona could see the depth of her transgressions against him and become remorseful. Maybe she'd say she was sorry and then leave them alone. It would be one way that his hurt and bitterness could dissolve.

He never considered himself to be the type to harbor bitterness. He thought he forgave Iona, only to find later he hadn't. The idea of trusting again seemed something he couldn't attain. He didn't want to become an angry, controlling man who had no ability to trust and forgive. He prayed again that God would help him and heal his life.

Creaking noises sounded from the bed again, and then the floor boards creaked. Maybe she'd decided to pace the floor or do exercises. Was his sleep only to be a fond memory?

Chapter 5

Greta awakened for the second or third time, but thankfully this time the sun was shining. She tumbled out of bed, feeling miserable and thirsty. After she showered, dressed, and drank a large glass of water, the lethargic feeling lessened. Breakfast would do the trick to make her feel better.

When she reached the dining room, not a soul was in sight, instead a sign and a box were on the bar counter. *Free Donuts for our Guests.* She opened the box and looked over the variety of glazed and cake donuts. How nice. She chose the one with pink frosting and took a bite. Next to the sign lay a hand written note. *Please join us at the corner church at nine thirty.* A smiley face with a halo decorated the right end corner.

She glanced at her watch. Nine thirty-five. She would've loved to have gone to an Irish church service. Having everyone's eyes on her as she walked in late would be too hard to take. It reminded her of bad dreams she had as a kid. But that was ridiculous. A few minutes late wouldn't be bad.

Even so, she turned around and headed back up to her room with the donut. She ate it as she climbed the stairs. Back safe in her room, she opened the bags from yesterday's shopping and pulled out a sketchpad and a corkboard.

She set the bulletin board flat on the table. Placing her tweed suitcase on the bed, she opened it up and carefully took out a zip lock bag of her favorite things, including notes from her mother.

She gently held a little card in the shape of a kitten. She couldn't bear to leave any of the precious things behind at home for Dad's girlfriend, Joanie, to gape at. Greta would only be at her dad's house for a short time until she found another apartment. But according to Joanie's eye-rolling, you'd think Greta was a bum intent on staying forever. She opened the card and reread the assurance from her mom. *I'll always love you.* A drawing of a tiger kitten hugging a heart decorated the inside. She'd place it on a top corner of the board.

The O'Riain's paper placemat with the scalloped edge peeked out of one of the bags. She smiled at the forlorn thing, and laid it on the board in the lower right hand corner. From her suitcase, she pulled out a container of thumb tacks and a roll of pink ribbon with black polka-dots and got to work.

After the bulletin board was complete, she set her attention on the sketch pad. All the ideas flowed easily onto the pages, and she felt a sense of accomplishment. They were part of the answer to getting more business to O'Riain's, and once the guests arrived, they'd be glad they came. At least that was the goal.

Even more, the work stimulated the artist in her. She'd thought she'd given up painting for good. For the art project that excited her the most, she needed a couple more pictures for reference.

She hurried down the steps with her camera. The empty dining tables and the closed kitchen door surprised her. No lunch either? Her stomach tightened. They weren't giving up already, were they? The box of donuts and sign were gone, but the handwritten note had drifted to the floor.

Spur of the moment, she tiptoed over, picked it up, and hurried back to the front entrance and out the door. Had Aedan written the note? If any of the O'Riains saw her pick it up, they'd think she was crazy. The smiley face was too good of a souvenir to let it be thrown away. She had an open spot on her bulletin board where it would slip right in.

She headed down the sidewalk on a mission to take pictures, the main subject being a cute critter by the name of Charles. Seeing the bench in the distance, she was not disappointed. A pine marten stood close to the older man.

"Hello again."

He nodded.

"Hope that I'm not bothering you."

"Not at all." He seemed to look around her as if she had a hidden white bag with sandwiches.

"Could I take a couple more pictures of Charles Dickens?"

"I don't think he'll mind."

She steadied her camera and snapped several pictures. The little brown animal sat and looked at her. It couldn't have been any more perfect. *Thank you, Lord.*

"Animals are wonderful, aren't they?" She wanted to touch the critter's fur.

"Aye, they are." He pressed his hat down further on his head. "Weren't you a bit nervous going alone for a walk today? With those scruffy types passing through town?"

"Not really, but I did feel a lot better when I saw you here. Do you live close by?"

"Er…um…" He paused as his eyes darted back and forth. "Actually, I'm just passing through.

"Oh?"

"But don't worry. I'm not like those young goats. My name is Finn Brody, and I guess you could say I'm on bit of a vacation—a bit of a time off."

****

Greta turned on the light in her darkening room and studied the pictures she had printed at a corner store. She chose one and pinned it on the bulletin board by a spot close to the smiley, then turned on the television.

She sat on the bed and clicked through channels as her mind drifted, taking a sip of Diet Coke from the petrol station. She felt good about the day— many things got accomplished, including the purchase of a phone to use in Ireland. She'd called every number on the list that could potentially lead to her biological father and scratched off twelve names. Five hadn't answered. Of the ones left to call, they were only listed as P. O'Cnaimhin. Almost certainly there wouldn't be a Padraig. Which was the more stressful, to find him or not find him?

She crossed her legs, and the movement made her notebook slip toward her. Picking it up, she paged through it, glad that she'd reviewed two more restaurants, one for lunch and one for dinner. They were both good, but not any real competition.

The thought of O'Riain's being closed for the day niggled in the back of her mind. Hopefully they'd be open tomorrow.

On the way back to her room from dinner, she'd heard footfalls on the stairs ahead of her and gotten a slight whiff of Aedan's cologne by the third floor. Had she just missed him by a second or two?

Why did she care so much about him and his family's struggle? Part of her interest had to be that she enjoyed a challenge. She wanted their business to succeed. It was ingrained in her as part of her profession. And the other part—providence?

She stepped over to view the new items on the

bulletin board and take in all the details. The overlapping arrangement of the Irish postcards over the O'Riain's Cottage placemat pleased her. If nothing else, color would help their design. Then she saw fine print close to the scalloped edge that she'd never seen before. *Closed Sundays*. Of course, that was Aedan's one day off.

Chapter 6

Excitement and a kind of dread filled Greta as she took her usual morning walk to see Charles Dickens. Her week was almost up, and she hadn't figured out a good plan on how to engage the O'Riains with her advertising strategies. She had to admit that having a place of business and a staff at her side bolstered her confidence. But all her clients came to her seeking help. She'd never chased after someone who thought advertising was a waste of time.

Her mind wandered as she strode along. Reece had invited her for dessert one evening, and she'd accepted. She smiled, envisioning his face light up as he told her about his all time favorite dishes made with fresh Irish ingredients. But he waggled a finger at her and said that he'd in no way give up secret recipes. Later that night as she was falling asleep, she thought she heard two male voices arguing again. She was too tired to care.

The next night, Aedan had taken her for a short evening walk, and they'd ventured into a pub to hear folk music. One of the songs was a dirge.

"A dirge?" she'd asked.

"Aye, it's a very sad song—a tragedy to help bring you back down if you happen to be *too* happy." His voice turned sarcastic, and the glare of his eyes could probably poke a hole in someone's hat.

She sat beside him at a table and laughed. "That's handy."

"To be sure. I know this one right off by the melody. It's a fisherman's wife, a wee lovely woman, looking for her husband. He's been lost at sea. She looks every morning and every evening to see if his poor body has washed ashore. All through her life until her hair grows white and her body thin. 'Dear Erin,' she calls, 'dear Erin.'" Then he sighed and mumbled.

Greta settled in her chair, not expecting much. The melody quickened and chords brought about a melancholy air. She knew music could portray sadness but not to this depth. She hung on the man's every word in the song. It gripped her heart. Somehow she became the wife searching for her lost love. The father of her dear sweet child. Tears formed in her eyes, and she wiped them away, only to be replaced by more. The song ended as the wee fisherman's wife was reunited with her Erin in death.

"Powerful." Aedan glanced in her direction.

"Aye." The answer slipped out.

His expression sparked for a split second as if in surprise or puzzlement, but she couldn't say anymore or she'd really start crying. Thank goodness the other songs became more cheerful as the man sang.

Aedan sipped his drink and relaxed. She guessed he wasn't kidding when he said he hardly ever got away from work. The change in him was like a heavy burden had been removed. His smile came easier that made his eyes happy, too.

After the songs were over, he kept the topics lighthearted, including everyday events, and she hadn't directed the conversation to anything deep or controversial. Although, she would've loved to have heard about Iona, and learned what she and Greta shared in looks. Their likeness to each other did make her nervous, since she was unsure about her biological father. What if Iona was a relative? Or even a sister or half sister, or dare she even consider it, a twin? The more she thought about it, the more it seemed possible. But was it her untrustworthy imagination?

Her thoughts were cut short when she stumbled on a small bump on the sidewalk. She glanced around and behind, no one around. What if Finn and Charles weren't there? She walked at a quicker pace as if that would make them appear.

She turned the slight bend in the path and saw Finn off in the distance, reading a newspaper. As she neared, Charles caught sight of her and kept his attention on her. He almost looked like he was smiling. She wished she could earn his trust enough, so she could pet him. Although, she'd never seen Finn touch the wild animal.

She'd brought fish sandwiches from O'Riain's since it was the lunch special for the day. She thought both the man and pine marten would enjoy the tasty food. In a cup carrier, she had two Cokes and a cup of water.

"What you have there?" Finn adjusted his hat.

"A surprise for you and Charles." She smiled.

Finn looked up and closed his eyes as if to offer a prayer of thanks while Charles dared to sniff the bag. She sat on the bench and ate with Finn while offering little bits of fish and a saucer of water to the pine marten.

"Well, my week of vacation at O'Riain's is up." She put her empty sandwich wrapper in the bag.

"That's the saddest news I've ever heard." Finn shook his head.

****

Greta wrestled with her thoughts in the afternoon and took a drive to Cork City. She ended up at a library and looked over a display of books. Cork cookbooks. She smiled at the American country cooking one. It ought to be in high demand, she thought sarcastically. Surprising it was still on the shelf. Home seemed so far and distant, like she'd been gone for months.

She headed for an internet connection and found a partitioned off room. A man approximately her age gave his undivided attention to his computer. She could have been wearing a red clown nose and he wouldn't have noticed. Poor guy was probably searching for a job. She set up her computer and accessed the internet, skimmed the page long email from Dad, and sent him a couple of lines to let him know that she was okay. Seriously, a whole page?

On the way out, she came across a board where people had pinned up information and business cards. Classes were offered in chess, computer, and drawing. She perused the signs and cards, each one a part of the person who put it there. Could she, per chance, make a living here?

What did Mom want her to experience here? A vacation? A life? When Greta had finally seen her birth certificate, her mother's words made total sense. Everything clicked into place that she was to find her biological father, but after going through the phone list, it seemed impossible. She heaved a heavy sigh that made one of the signs flutter. He might not be alive. Could be she was too late.

Greta stepped out of the library, thinking she'd go to a courthouse and find public records, then stopped and turned around. She'd do a search on the internet.

****

Greta sat in her usual chair for dinner and a tingle of happiness swept over her when Aedan came to take her order. As soon as he saw her, he sauntered her direction. He totally meant to tease her with the way he walked. His smile wasn't completely hidden by his hand as he cleared this throat.

"Miss Greta, what can I get you tonight?"

She waited, breathlessly looking into his eyes.

"The special tonight is...smoked salmon served with an artisanal flat bread, Greek salad, and complimentary dessert later with...Aedan?" His voice became softer with each passing word.

When she didn't reply, he leaned closer. "Or would you rather go somewhere else in town? I know of—"

"I'd love to, but I'm sorry, I can't." She hated turning him down.

His puzzled expression asked her to explain.

"It's...my last night here. I need to make plans to figure out—"

"You're last night?" Relief washed over him, then he snapped to attention. "Sorry, I—"

"That's okay." Really it was all right, but it hurt knowing he was glad to see her go. Her resemblance to Iona probably killed any friendship they could possibly have. She grabbed her purse and stood to leave.

"Wouldn't you like dinner?"

"Uh—no. Thanks. Well—good night." She hastily turned to leave and broke eye contact.

She wished she would've turned to see his face one more time, but she left the dining area with her only goal to get to her room. What difference did it make if she ever saw him again? He was relieved to see her go. Why had she ever thought she could help the family with their business? It was a silly pipedream that she could make any difference—foolish to think that Aedan liked her.

When she reached her room, she wiped tears from her eyes, angry that it bothered her so much. She really felt that God had led her to this place to do something good in the O'Riain's lives. If only Aedan had appeared sad when she said she was leaving instead of smiling like he won a vacation.

But it shouldn't matter if Aedan liked her or not. If God wanted her to help them, shouldn't she set her feelings aside and help them?

She wrapped herself up in the handmade quilt, stretched out on the bed, and prayed for direction. Her thoughts drifted and her eyes closed.

Voices jostled her from sleep. Minutes if not hours must've passed. Two men talked in hushed tones. Her eyelids became heavy once more, but then fluttered open at the sound of a woman crying. Had to be Aedan's mom...Alice. Greta pictured his mother's pink nametag. What could've happened?

"...with Liam gone." Alice's voice.

"We'll have to get a replacement. That's all we can do." Aedan's voice came through with reassurance. "You can't expect the poor man to turn down a better paying job in Cork."

"I know. I know. But he didn't give us any notice. I don't want to hire someone who will turn the customers away. The person has to be a cheerful, hard-working soul."

"Aye."

"How can we find this person in no time at all? It would have to be a miracle. Plus another guest is leaving tomorrow...your Greta."

"She's not my Greta."

"Just to make the bare minimum we need, another guest has to come and come right away. I don't know. Aedan, it looks like we've finally come to the end of all things."

"No, Ma."

Alice cried and blew her nose. "Aye. It is. You'd better pray."

"I will."

"And you'd better pray that I won't have a fitful sleep. I feel a bad dose of the flu coming on. Then what will we do?"

Aedan replied, but Greta couldn't quite make out the words. She struggled to hear more, but the voices were too hushed. After a short while, she gave up and snuggled into bed even though she wasn't a bit sleepy. A restless night seemed inevitable.

****

Aedan wiped a clean, hot washcloth over his face then stepped over to his door, listened, and locked it for good measure. Was everyone in the world touched in the head, leaving him the only sane one left? His family was driving him crazy. Ma cried at any hint of disaster, and Reece was determined to pursue Greta. If Aedan turned completely bonkers, he'd fit right in. He rolled his eyes and hit his temple with the heel of his hand. No problems then.

He slipped out of his work clothes and yanked on his flannel pants. He fairly crawled to his bed, he was so tired. He covered up and closed his eyes. Creaking sounds permeated the floor above him as Greta moved. Fantastic. *Dear Lord, thank you that she's leaving tomorrow. Maybe I can get some sleep soon.* Oh. Wrong. He wasn't supposed to pray that. He was supposed to pray for a new waiter and a lodging guest. Plus no dose of the flu for Ma. *Please, dear Lord, take care of that.*

A wave of fatigue nearly slapped him silly. Even the creakin' and squeakin' couldn't possibly keep him awake.

He'd probably been asleep for an hour or two when the noise started up again. Not enough to wake him up but enough to add interest to his dream of being stuck on the high seas, rocking back and forth in the belly of an old wooden ship.

Sunlight drifted in the window warning him of the passing time. He opened one eye to look at the clock and jumped in disbelief. "No—how did?"

"Aedan." Ma pounded at the door.

"Coming. I'll be right down." He jumped out of bed.

"Okay. But since you slept in, you missed all the news." Her voice floated through the door.

Chapter 7

Aedan couldn't decipher from Ma's voice if the news was good or bad. He hurried to get ready for the day, showered, trimmed his beard, and yanked on clean clothes. A look in the mirror told him he'd be suitable to meet a police sergeant, collection agency personnel, or a colonoscopy doctor. Either way he was sure to be run through the wringers. Aye, even good enough to meet the coroner. He took in a deep breath and an eyelid twitched.

Wait a minute. If it were bad news, Ma would be crying her eyes out. The news either had to be good news or just so-so news.

When he reached the kitchen, he took a quick once over of the breakfast guests. Every group was eating. Great. He grabbed the coffee pot to offer more, when Reece stepped into the kitchen with Greta. Each had a big smile and laughed at some unknown joke. Aedan almost lost his grip on the pot and steadied it with his other hand, burning his fingers. He was already upset at seeing the two being all buddy-buddy, and getting burned was like sticking a mad bull with a pin.

"Reece." The name came out louder than he intended. He took in a breath to compose himself. "Reece, what's going on? Why do we have a guest in the kitchen?"

His brother laughed and slapped him on the back. "She's no guest."

A movement off to Aedan's right caught his attention. Their mother appeared. "Ma?" His insides churned. He must look like a complete eejit.

"Here, set the coffee pot down for a minute." Ma took it away from him. His eejit status just multiplied. She nodded to Greta. "We have a new waitress who can also help in the kitchen."

"What?" *Unbelievable.* "You...you're..." He sought some sort of information from Greta. His thoughts couldn't mesh together to make a sentence. Her amazing red hair glowed fiery copper where a patch of sun warmed it.

"I'm going to help out for two weeks until you find someone." Greta's calm words touched him. Her voice was like sweet nectar or something tangible that he needed to mend a wound.

The anger melted away. She was only going to stay a bit longer. Then everything would return back to normal—whatever that was.

"Someone headed to the front desk to check in. I'll go see to it." Ma set off in a full stride. She turned back and pointed at him. "Now, Aedan, don't you be too hard on her."

He shook his head. "No worries." He picked up the coffee pot again and set out on his own mission.

After everyone had been offered more coffee, Aedan made his way to the front desk.

"There you go Mr. Brody. Your room is right around the corner there on the first floor. Room one-oh-seven." Ma handed him a key.

"Thank you, Ma'am." The older man tipped his hat.

"Are you sure now that you aren't a famous actor?" She giggled and touched his elbow.

"I'm sure." He chuckled. "It's just me. Just Finn."

Aedan smiled, amused at their banter. "Have a good day."

"Oh, I will. I will." He tipped his hat again and headed toward his room.

"Things are looking up again." Her eyes sparkled. "And even better than before."

"Now wait. What's all this about Greta working for us?"

"Oh, it's a pitiful story. I do say."

"What?"

"Greta said there was some sort of thing, and she wondered if she could work for us in exchange for her room and meals. She really is a sweet girl."

"But she's Iona."

"Hmm? I don't think so."

"Isn't it taking a big chance? What if she has

plans to ruin—"

"That young woman wouldn't hurt anything."

"But—"

"Ah, would ya get out of that garden. Everything's going to be fine."

As long as Ma thought so, maybe he should run with it. They'd certainly had enough crying for a while. "Okay, then."

To protect Reece, the only thing Aedan could do was woo Greta. That is, if she was still willing after getting all his brother's attention.

Aedan made his way back to the kitchen and found Reece showing Greta how to prepare a potato pancake. The hearty side dish was on the schedule for tomorrow's special.

Reece glanced up, and his eyes sparked as he smiled. "Just showing Greta how to prepare boxty. It will help to be a jump ahead, if she knows how to prepare it."

"It would." He was like a balloon that lost all its air, but that was much better than a raging bull. If his brother was going to capture Greta's heart or vise versa, there wasn't much Aedan could do about now. Not that he'd give up.

"It will give us something to eat for breakfast," his brother said to Greta. "Oh, and you too." Reece shot him a glance.

He didn't bother to answer. Right now he didn't care if he ate or not. "I'll go clean the tables."

When he returned with the dirty dishes, Greta had a stack of boxty on a large platter and placed another one with the group. The smell of the golden fried potatoes, enticing.

"There was a rhyme, when Aedan and I were growing up. The girls would tease each other with it. Something about if you don't eat boxty, you'll never get a man." Reece chuckled.

Greta took a sharp intake of breath. "Oh my goodness. That must be my problem."

"Well, here you go." Reece handed her a plate and fork. "Problem solved."

She giggled and Aedan forgot for a split second that she was Iona. He wished he could've been the one to tell her about the rhyme and make her laugh.

"Now, Greta, I'm sure you've had many a man after you," Aedan said.

"I've never let him catch me, I guess."

Reece's jaw dropped.

"I mean, I'd be married if I did, and I'm not." Greta took a bite.

Aedan lost all his air and tried to hide his face while rinsing the plates. Really nice of her to make light of leaving him at the altar. She had to think they were completely fooled by the American accent and her changes in appearance.

Reece had insisted that Greta join him at a booth near the kitchen to eat breakfast. She ate the last bite of the fried potato cakes from her plate. Delicious and satisfying.

"So you think I'll be able to help tomorrow with the special?"

"I'm sure of it." Reece looked back to the kitchen.

"Is something bothering Aedan? He didn't seem like himself."

"He's probably just tired. We've been on a tough schedule. But we don't want your schedule to be long like ours, so why not take a break and meet me back in the kitchen at four."

"But I can help at lunch, too."

"Well, at least come to eat."

"Uh—"

"If we're completely run over, then you can help. I doubt that will happen."

"Has business been running a little slow?"

"Aye. I can say it has."

"Have you tried advertising…at all?"

"Advertising? Like throwing money down a hole, it is. No, we won't have anything to do with it."

Exactly a response she expected.

"Word of mouth has always been the best…well…for getting the word out." He nodded and stood up, grabbing their empty plates.

"The pork roast you made was the best I've ever had. I'm sure to tell everyone I know and maybe even ones I don't know." She stood and patted his arm.

"Done with breakfast?" Aedan joined them and noticed her hand on Reece's arm. She was almost certain it caused him to frown. A surprising action coming from one who was relieved to see her go. Maybe she'd misread him before. What did he really think?

"I'll do the clean up." Reece's expression turned serious as if in concern for Aedan. "Anyone that comes in before lunch—I've got it. There's precious little to be done to prepare for the lunch crowd. Go get some rest for an hour."

"Okay, but what about Greta. You shouldn't work her to death. She's still our guest."

"She's coming back to help us at dinner." Reece gave her a wink.

"Good enough." Aedan walked out of the dining room with her and waved to his mom, Alice, on the way out.

"I hope you don't mind that I'm helping out. It was so kind of your mother to let me work for room and board," Greta said, hoping to glean any sort of clue as to what he thought.

"It's fine—fine." He nodded and started up the stairs ahead of her.

Thank you, Lord. It worked out so well. All the money she would've used went to Finn, so he could stay at O'Riain's for two weeks. His almost teary-eyed expression of gratitude made the whole trip worthwhile. If the O'Riains wouldn't accept her help with advertising, at least she brought some happiness to the older man. It fulfilled her desire to help someone in honor of her mother. If she could do even more, all the better.

She wracked her brains to think of any topic, but it seemed he didn't want to talk.

On the first landing, he bent over to pick up a scrap of paper and a ripping sound let loose. A large tear appeared in the back of his pants revealing red plaid material. He turned to look and quickly covered the spot with his hand. "Oh, blimey."

She couldn't choke back her giggle quick enough. "I'm sorry."

He chuckled. "I guess it's way overdue. These

pants are as old as the hills. Well, not quite…but close. Guess I'll be spending time mending instead of resting."

"I'll sew them for you."

"I can't expect y—"

"Really. I'll do it. I have a sewing kit. I'd be happy to."

He sighed. "All right then. I'm so tired; I'd probably stitch them into a knot. Follow me."

"Okay, boss." Wherever he led, she'd follow. Well, almost.

On the third floor, he unlocked a main door. "This is our home."

"Nice."

The walls were in a light muted tan and the carpeting a deep brown. The colors exuded a relaxed feeling. Any troubles were swept away. She was sure the ones who lived here needed all the rest they could get. To the right was a dark wood table covered with a light green tablecloth and surrounded by six chairs. She imagined herself sitting there with a cup a tea and then meandering to the windows to look down on the street.

A tidy kitchen with polished metal appliances and a breakfast bar was beyond the table. To the left was a tranquil living room with overstuffed furniture in chocolate brown. The windows on that side of their home showed a view of a yard and trees, neighboring homes, and in the distance was the ocean.

One thing struck her as odd. There weren't any pictures or wall decorations. Nothing on the table or even the coffee table in the living room. Just wide open space. Maybe that's what the family needed after working constantly with the clatter and commotion of customers.

"I'll be right back." He headed off with his hand covering his pants and gave a backward glance to her with a hesitant smile.

His room being on the corner explained a lot. It had to be right under hers. He opened the dark brown door, stepped inside the room, and closed the door with a click.

While she waited, she stepped to the living room windows to enjoy the scenery. The space was well kept with a garden and a bench. Possibly a new bench for Finn and Charles. A movement caught her eye. She stifled a giggle as Finn tried out the bench and rested an arm over the back. No sign of Charles. The little pine marten probably wouldn't want to venture that far into town.

Her gaze wandered to the horizon. The blue, sparkling ocean appeared beyond the trees. She relaxed her shoulders, not knowing that she'd held her muscles so tight.

A clunk sounded from a door.

"Well, here we go—oh wait." Aedan's voice came from the hall.

She walked over to meet him there and saw him disappear into his bedroom again. He'd put on some sweatpants and had his black pants under an arm. Reaching his door, she caught a glimpse in his room.

"Oh—" Her fingers covered her lips. His bedroom was a storage room. Paintings and pictures stood against the walls and knick-knacks covered any flat space available. Boxes were stacked against a far wall by his bed, the same size of hers upstairs.

"Here. I wanted to give you payment for the mending." He put a handful of euro coins in her palm, equal to about eight dollars.

"Oh, no." She shook her head. "I don't want—"

"Please." His eyes implored her then glanced around his room.

"I can't. You don't even know what kind of job I'll do." She winced and handed back the money.

"Okay. But I'll make it up to you somehow." He set the coins on a dresser and stepped out of his room as he closed the door behind him. "Sorry you had to see the bealin' mess."

She waved and shook her head. "No problem."

"When Da died last year with a heart attack, Ma didn't want to see our home the way it used to be. She wanted a change. We swapped our furniture out and repainted." He motioned to his room with a jerk of his thumb. "She wanted to get rid of everything. It didn't bother Reece, but...I couldn't let go of everything. Da's memories are mixed with it."

"I understand."

He blinked then looked away and led her back through the house.

"My mom..."

He turned in her direction as he opened the main door.

"She passed away when I was young." Greta stepped through the door.

"I'm sorry. Had to be terrible. How did she...?"

"Drunk driver...hit her." She was uncertain of how much to tell him. Hard to believe that her mom while in a coma told Greta to go to Cork. She believed it to be a miracle. How could she expect anyone else to understand?

Aedan leaned against the door jam. He seemed to study her expression, but his eyes were gentle.

"She's the main reason why I'm here…why I came to Ireland. I…I'm trying to find my biological father." Greta's lip trembled and her eyes became blurry. If only she'd learned how to play poker, so she could've learned how to have a poker face.

"How is your search coming?"

"I found a list of names from a directory. Got in touch with all except two. They either don't want to answer the phone, or aren't there. I guess it's a long shot that either of them could be my father."

"What's his name?"

"Padraig O'Cnaimhin."

"That's an old Irish name for sure."

She looked at the bundle he held.

He handed her the pants. "They…um…are the only clean ones I have. If I could have them back…?"

"I'll work on it right away. Want to pick them up a few minutes before you head back to work?"

"Perfect. And about your da, I hope you can find him."

Aedan headed back to his room and stretched out on the bed. Greta looking for her father put on a whole new turn. At first the story of her ma dying when she was little seemed to be something that Iona had cooked up to play with his feelings. But the tears and quivering lower lip had to be authentic. The more she talked, the more the story rang true. A young woman searching for her da. A female who looked exactly like his ex.

Could she be Iona's sister even though the last names didn't match up? The man could've changed his name. If Iona's father was her da, she'd be disappointed. Maybe it would be better not to find out.

He rolled over on his side and tried to push everything from his mind.

But if Iona made up the story...no. He wasn't going to go there. He would only think of her as Greta Conner, because that's who she had to be. His bad feelings against Iona had clouded his vision against Greta, and he wasn't about to let it happen anymore. Besides that, all the bitterness had dissolved. All the bad emotions—nonexistent.

Greta's look of pure delight as she ate the chocolate cake came to mind. The sweetness of her laugh. Then at the pub listening to the folk singer with the sad song. He was touched that she could be brought to such sorrow over someone else's heartache. To feel empathy for another.

He loved her kind, gentle spirit. It must be genuine. No way to fake that.

What had happened to bring her financial trouble? Whatever it was, he was almost glad for it. He'd get to work with her and see her for two more weeks. Why he had a thing for redheads, he'd never know.

Aye, he was thankful for his split pants, too. Hearing her laughter at the embarrassing predicament, uplifted his spirits. And her kindness for mending them had done something to him.

When she took his pants, she might as well have taken his heart, too.

Chapter 8

Aedan knocked on Greta's door, and when it opened, he blinked and looked again. On the table sat a painted canvas surrounded by tubes of paint and brushes. Against the wall stood a board with all sorts of things pinned to it. "Hello. Looks like you have an art studio."

"Hope you don't mind." She held his work pants under an arm.

"Not at all. Mind if I take a gander?"

"Please." She smiled and gave a little nod, then stepped aside so he could enter. As he neared the canvas, she said, "It's a—"

"Pine marten." He looked at her glowing expression. "You're an artist."

"It's been a long time since I've painted."

"I like it. I like it a lot." How surprising to learn of her talent. He glanced at the varied things on the bulletin board. "Is that to help with ideas for other paintings?"

"They're favorite things that I like to keep near and look at." She stepped closer to it, and he followed. She pointed to cards for a child. "Those were from my mom. And the handwritten quotes are hers, oh, and the calligraphy."

"Impressive." The lettering flowed in a perfect Celtic style. "Didn't you say you like the *Book of Kells*? I bet you got that from your ma."

"Yes, I was hoping that I'd get to see it when I'm here, but guess it will have to be another time."

"So was she Irish or—"

"American. But came here to live for a couple of years. I heard from my aunt that she loved Ireland and wanted to live here, but she promised her family she'd come back."

"There's an Irish proverb that your feet will take you where your heart is."

"That's so fitting. Mom loved two places— Ireland and America." She glanced at the pants she held. "Oh. Here."

"Thank you. It helps a lot. And I was able to get some rest, too."

"Great."

"Well, carry on." He motioned to the painting.

"I've got a couple more canvases to work on, some square ones."

"Can't wait to see them." He backed into the corner of the door, making a thudding noise. *Ouch!*

"See you at four." All he needed to do was rip another hole.

She nodded, smiled her pretty smile, and waved. Aye, all of her smiles were pretty.

He hurried down the hallway and jogged down the steps to his room. Yanked off the sweat pants and started to put on the pants. The seam was sewn neatly in uniform tiny stitches. That her hands had mended something for him warmed his heart. How was he going to keep Reece from stealing her away from him? Reece had all the good looks plus all the good cooking skills, too.

He headed down to the kitchen to help with prep work. And it was about time to get more carnations. That would make Ma happy. What could he get for Greta?

"Why are you grinning? What's so funny?" Reece held a potato he was scrubbing.

"Me? Nothing." He didn't even know he was smiling.

"I was thinking."

"No."

"I didn't even tell you yet." Reece frowned. "I'm going to ask Greta if she'll get a drink with me after work."

"Sorry. She already has plans."

"With you?"

"Aye. With me. And it's going to stay that way." He thought Reece started to snicker, but he turned his head away from him as he grabbed more potatoes to wash.

"Ha. Well. I *hope* you have a whale of a time." Reece's tone was a bit sarcastic.

"Since you don't need help, I'm off to get fresh carnations."

"Ma was wondering. It's not good to keep her wondering."

Really? Was it ever good to keep any woman wondering?

****

Greta finished painting three of the ten inch square canvases with Irish countryside scenes. A nice grouping of them displaced by the front entrance would be interesting. The colors of green landscapes would look fresh and clean, contrasting with the peach colored wall. Would Aedan like it? The blank walls begged for some sort of decoration. But perhaps that was the way Alice preferred it.

After a quick glance at the time, Greta headed out of her room. As she stepped out, a pink color caught her eye. A rose in a vase sat by her door. She picked it up and smelled the sweet fragrance. A note was tied to it and signed with a smiley face. *Thank you for my mending.* She smelled the delicate flower again, took it inside her room, and set it on the nightstand.

When she arrived in the kitchen, Aedan and Reece seemed to be having a disagreement. What it was she couldn't determine. They quieted down the minute she appeared.

"Hey, there. What can I do?" She looked first to Aedan then Reece.

"A family just seated. Go with Aedan and pick up his awesome technique of taking an order." Reece rolled his eyes.

Aedan picked up the paper and pen. "Have a good afternoon?"

"I did." After stepping out of earshot from Reece, she leaned close as they walked. "Thank you for the beautiful flower."

"You're welcome. Want to go out after work?" he said in a hushed voice.

She nodded and could imagine her eyes sparkled with happiness as she smiled.

Her thoughts went back and forth, wondering what he had planned. An evening walk, tea with quiet conversation, or go to one of the pubs? When he greeted the family and took their drink order, she set the excited thoughts aside.

During the early evening, Greta realized that she enjoyed being a waitress. Working with the two men was a pleasure, too. They accepted her and liked her.

She also loved the Irish accent of the guests. It seemed to make everything lighthearted. Even when negative things were said, the words were so unusual that they lost their weight. The phrases were amusing instead of angry.

When the last of the guests were gone and the kitchen cleaned, she looked in Aedan's direction with an unspoken question.

"I'll pick you up at your place in about fifteen," Aedan said.

"Oh. Nice. I'd ask if I can come along but—" Reece exaggerated his words in sorrow and heaved a heavy sigh.

Aedan slapped him on the back. "Don't worry. Someday your true love will come along."

Reece's eyes widened, and then he let a whoop of laughter. "Oh, aye, brother."

"It's been a long day. No wonder my words came out arseways." Aedan's face took on a reddish tone.

She could only hope her face didn't match his in color.

****

Aedan glanced at the passenger seat where Greta sat. He guessed she didn't mind too much about being assigned the designation of his true love and was still willing to go sightseeing with him. Driving in the car at night did help in some ways. At least she wouldn't be able to see his face turn red if he played the part of an eejit again.

"You and your brother get along well."

"Ah, sure look it." He wasn't sure how to respond.

"You don't?"

"We do, I suppose. As kids though..." He shook his head. "We drove Ma to distraction."

"Your personalities clashed? That's how it was for me and my brother."

"Not really. We were competitive. We each wanted to outdo the other. Besides that, Reece was a trickster. An evil mastermind, he was."

She laughed. "Oh, no. What did he do?"

"He would devise some disaster and pin it on me."

"And he got away with it?"

"Not all the time. Once Da got wise to him, Reece didn't have much of a chance. And Da would remind him of it every time he thought Reece was up to no good. He called him the…" Aedan tried to hold back a chuckle. "He called him the *flat tire* of the family." He threw his head back and laughed.

"That is hilarious. Why?" She giggled. The silhouette of her red hair glowed in the moonlight. Her face still visible in the faint light had a pleasant expression.

"Reece was about thirteen at the time and ticked at me. I was supposed go to a meeting with Da. I don't even remember what it was, some dull thing. Anyway, Reece didn't like it that I got to go and he didn't, so before a friend picked him up, he let the air out of a front tire. He hid the tire pump and spare tire, then took off.

"But we didn't know that he'd done it. Da saw the flat tire and thought he'd run over a nail. He shrugged his shoulders and said that we could walk. Only a few blocks, it was. The meeting was so long and terrible to sit through, I thought I'd go crazy. When we got home, Ma said that Reece called and needed a ride home.

"Uh, oh."

"Aye, right. There was no way to fix the tire to go get him. He had to walk home. Twelve kilometers…about six miles. Took him about two and a half hours to get home. Guess he didn't count on that. Next morning before everyone woke up, the tire was fixed and everything back in place."

"Did he admit to doing it then?"

"Not right away. And when he did, he laughed over Da's puzzled expression about the reappearing tire pump and the fixed tire." Aedan chuckled. "It was a gas."

"Uh, huh." She smiled.

"I guess you had to be there. Anyway the nickname stuck, and Da used it whenever anything remotely fishy happened. I can still hear Da's voice saying, 'It looks like the flat tire has been a thumping by.'"

"You ever call him that?"

He choked on a short laugh. "Never. It was Da's thing. Good that Reece hasn't done anything lately."

"Guess he's outgrown being a trickster."

"Maybe not. If it's part of his personality, it's lying dormant, festering to come out. Scary thought that." He stopped the car in front of a gate.

"Where are we?"

"Old Head. One of me favorite places." A peace came over him. He'd made the right decision bringing her here.

The gatekeeper stepped to the driver's side. "Name?"

"Aedan O'Riain."

The man flipped through several papers. "Hold on." He opened the gate and motioned them through.

The car proceeded through the gate and the land narrowed with cliffs and ocean on either side.

Greta looked out her window. "Whoa."

"Don't worry. We won't go over the edge."

"No…I mean this place is amazing."

"Used to come here as a kid—anyone could come. Then it became closed to the public for a golf course. A childhood friend of mine is a member, and he put me on the list. Otherwise…well…" He couldn't bring himself to finish the sentence. "How about a short walk?"

"I'd love to. Thanks for bringing me here. Ireland is so beautiful."

"It is. I'll never grow tired of it."

"Just the few things I've painted, I feel like I could keep painting scenes here for the rest of my life. I thought I'd never paint again."

"Really, now?"

She gave a short nod. A look of pain flitted across her face.

"What made you stop painting?" He almost regretted his question. If it was bad enough to stop the creative process, it was probably too hard to talk about. But his curiosity wouldn't let it be.

Chapter 9

Greta inhaled a slow, long breath and tried to relax. After all, she'd inadvertently brought up the subject. It was a perfectly normal question for him to ask.

"I'm sorry. You don't have to answer if—"

She waved the words away. "It's okay. I became disillusioned with my career. I hated everything about the direction my life was going." She made a thb sound with her lips and used the thumbs down signal.

The expression must have tickled him; a smile crept to his face.

She continued, "Nothing happened the way it was planned."

"Ah, you could be telling my story."

"Art was my whole life growing up. I couldn't wait to see yearly shows that would come to town and see my favorite artists or discover new ones. I studied, practiced, and practically breathed drawing and painting. In college, I got my bachelor's in fine art. I met my soul mate there, and we became engaged. I believed God made us for each other. We were going to have our own business, and we planned to join the artists in the shows that traveled across the country."

Aedan steered the car into a parking place and turned off the engine. He looked as though he held his breath, waiting.

"Then a friend told me news I didn't want to hear."

His eyes focused on her gently with sympathy.

"He had another girlfriend…a relationship almost the whole time I knew him. He'd given her an engagement ring, too."

"The manky git." He rolled the words off his tongue in a hushed voice.

"Everything collapsed on itself. My whole life how I'd dreamed it to be…ruined. Giving up art was my way of grieving. I'd promised myself that I'd never paint again. Letting it go was almost freeing because that part of my life was over."

"But now—"

"Now I feel different inside. And it's a good feeling. I have the desire to create again."

"I'm glad you came here." He sighed.

"Me too, it's made a big difference in my outlook on life."

He put his hand on top of hers. "Shall we go?"

"It looks...intriguing." More that it looked frightening in the shadowy dark. But at least Aedan knew the surroundings. The place had to be safe.

He abruptly let go of her hand and headed out of the car. He met her at her car door as she stepped out. The wind tugged at her hair and the sound of waves crashing intensified.

"The ocean rushing against the shore is mesmerizing." She held back her hair from her face.

"Very calming, it is. But at night, to be truthful, it seems a bit scary." He smiled.

As they walked a shadowy image appeared in the not too far distance. In the moonlight and patches of fog it seemed to crouch down to make an attack, then stood again. Or didn't it move?

"Is that a person up ahead...or—" A cold sensation of fear swept down her spine.

He stopped dead in his tracks. "Oh, no. Watch out!" His voice was urgent, fearful.

"What?" She stood as close as she could to him, clutching his arm. She searched the menacing figure for any movement and psyched herself up either to fight or run. But running sounded like a much better option.

He made a choking noise, alarming her all the more, and then a chuckle sneaked out. "It's a rock. Actually, it's called—" He laughed again. "—the Stone of Accord."

She let go of his arm. "Aedan O'Riain. You scared me to death."

"Sorry. I couldn't help it." He rubbed her shoulder as if to console her.

"I thought it was a person with a pointy hood."

"The night and fog can play tricks with your eyes."

He led her to the rock. The closer they got, she could see a round hole went completely through it.

"I suppose if you stare hard enough at the hole a fairy will appear." She stepped closer to the rock and peered through.

"No. *Not here*." He smiled and walked around to the other side and put his hand near the opening. "Take hold of my hand."

The evening had taken on such a dream like quality that she had to remind herself it was real. The rock was real, rough and cold. Aedan and his voice were real. She took hold of his warm hand and held it.

"There we go. It's done." He let go of her hand.

"What's done?"

"We're quingled by the Stone of Accord of Ireland."

"Ah—what? We're married?"

"Oh. You know what quingled means. Can't get anything past you." He came around the rock formation and gave her a light hug. His warmth and masculine, spicy scent made her wish he hadn't stepped away.

"But I never said, 'I do.'"

"Blimey! I forgot that part. I guess it didn't take then. But…at least we're friends?"

"Yes. We're good friends. There's something about you." She squinted an eye at him to tease him, not meaning anything in particular. She held back a giggle.

"What now?"

Keep him on his toes, Greta.

The ocean waves swept against the shoreline and the moonlight sparkled a path in the water. A breeze ruffled his hair as if someone came and tousled it and said, 'Now, here's a good boy.'

"I'm glad that you came to O'Riain's—glad that I met you." He paused as he seemed to search her eyes. "You're a *fine thi*—woman." He stepped closer.

So he thought she was beautiful...?

"Aw, away on that." She smiled at the chance to use an Irish phrase, but maybe it wasn't the right phrase.

"Want to grab some chips?"

"Chips at this hour?"

"Aye, of course. I know a place." He smiled.

As she walked with him to his car, he took her hand and held it. "Just to be on the safe side. Can't have you go slipping down into a hole or something."

"Thoughtful of you, to be sure." She tried to mimic his speech pattern, but without the Irish brogue. Her thoughts went to Iona. Had Aedan brought her here many a time? "I hate to ask, but…"

The faint smile still on his face didn't waver. "Ask anyway."

"Has the Stone of Accord…um." Why didn't she think before she spoke? "Has it seen the likes of Iona many of time?"

Taking in a sharp breath, he said, "Thank the Lord, I never brought her here."

"Really?"

He shook his head. "I didn't. This isn't her idea of a good time."

"Oh." Somehow the answer both relieved her and upset her. What was Iona's idea of a good time? She absolutely hated to ask that.

****

Next morning, Greta woke up before her alarm and headed down early to help with breakfast. Reece stood in front of the coffee maker as if he could will the machine to work faster.

"Where's Aedan?"

"Good morning to you, too," Reece said flatly. "He'll be down."

"Great. And Alice?" She looked around for their mother. She always busied herself, cleaning with a small cloth.

"Who—oh you mean Ma." Reece grinned at her.

"Yeah." Greta could only imagine that she had a perplexed expression on her face.

"Let me explain." He said in a hushed voice. "Ma's name really isn't Alice. She found the name tag and likes to wear it. I guess she must like the name, too."

"So what's her name?" She quieted her voice to a whisper to match his.

"Oh, no. She wouldn't be a letting us tell her name. As far as you know, it's Alice—at least this week unless she finds another name tag she likes better."

"O—kay."

Footfalls sounded near the kitchen, and Greta looked toward the doorway feeling a little guilty. Why she felt guilty, she had no idea. Maybe it was all the whispering, and she'd leaned on Reece in order to hear him. At least it wasn't Alice coming through the doorway.

"What's the story?" Aedan looked at his brother who grinned and then at Greta who could melt through the floor. She inched away from Reece.

Reece had a way of making everything look totally different with just one little expression. He smirked and lifted a shoulder as if to say, it's none of your business. She guessed the trickster part of him was still there—that thumping flat tire.

Greta felt uncomfortable as her cheeks were probably turning red. What did Aedan think? His expression turned serious, and he folded his arms across his chest. What did he think they were talking about—or what did he think they'd done? Who knew? But one thing was sure. She was innocent yet projecting an aura of guilt.

"Nothing. There's no story." She finally spoke the words that came to mind and then whispered. "Reece was telling me about your mom's nametag."

"It will be a blessing for us all if she finds one she likes and sticks to it. She's always looking for a better—"

"Sticks to what? What's sticky?" Alice stepped into the kitchen with her cleaning rag."

"It's okay, Ma. We've got." Reece nodded.

"Just so you do. And I've got good news. We signed on two more families to stay with us for a week."

"Great." Reece answered as Aedan moved to stand closer to Greta.

"That's not all. When they noticed how surprised I was—really, I tried to tone it down—both families mentioned that they read about our place in a *bog*." Alice shook her head as she said the word. "How could that possibly work?"

"A bog?" Aedan's eyes widened.

"They mean a *blog*. You know, a page on the internet where people write about their experiences...and everyone, who wants to, can read them." Greta couldn't help explaining. How wonderful that someone saw her comments about O'Riain's. She'd have to get a website going soon.

"But how did that happen?" Alice asked.

"I typed out a few good things about O'Riain's on some blogs about vacations. Or could be they saw someone else's comments." Greta smiled and envisioned a couple of ads.

"You see there. I was right. Word of mouth is always the best advertising." Alice set her lips in a grim line.

Greta gritted her teeth. Maybe her helpful plan had a way of backfiring. She sighed and tried with all her concentration not to roll her eyes. Since she had all three of the family in one room, she needed to spring at least one of her ideas on them. The least threatening one. Baby steps.

"Another way to get people to notice O'Riain's Cottage is visually along with word of mouth. The more avenues you have the better." Greta tried to speak matter-of-factly, but she couldn't keep the rise of excitement out of her voice.

Alice's eyes narrowed somewhat. "What do you mean?"

"People can talk about Reece's fabulous cooking…"

"That's right. I'm sure they do," Alice said.

"But what if those people aren't nearby? How about a chalkboard sign outside that tells about the specials for the day? That way anyone walking by could see it and become interested in giving it a try."

"Don't we have one of those signs with an easel?" Aedan opened a lower cupboard door. "I think it's a fantastic idea. Why didn't we keep it up?"

"I know. I got stuck with writing it out. People complained that they couldn't read my writing." Reece frowned.

"I'll do the lettering and design for you." Greta gave a little jump. Enthusiasm for the project bubbled inside. Aedan pulled out a chalkboard and a variety of chalk. He gave her a wink then looked at his mother. A slow smirk appeared on the older woman's face.

Then Greta knew. Reece had to have gotten the sneaky, trickster gene from his mom. What was she thinking? Did the crooked smile mean that she liked the idea? Or that she was the one who thought about it in the first place?

Chapter 10

Greta got the word from Reece about the special of the day. She sketched out the wording on a scrap of paper to get the layout how she wanted. Then started on the chalkboard with a piece of lime-green chalk. She was on her third day of writing out the fancy script. When Aedan saw her chalk lettering on the first day, he'd acted as excited about it as she felt inside. The best part was that it worked. More people came to eat at O'Riain's.

"Do you think those specials will draw people in today?" Reece stood by her left elbow.

"I don't see why not. Desserts are always a special treat."

"But a main course isn't listed."

"You do have a point there. How about if the special is the price...for the fish and chips? Then list the desserts afterward?"

"That's a grand idea. They'll get the special price, and be tempted by the afters."

Aedan appeared on her right. "You have a true gift. Your paintings have added to the atmosphere of the place."

"You really like them?" Greta hoped he meant it and wasn't just saying that to be kind.

"Yes, if only—"

"We have a family ready for breakfast." Reece interrupted.

"I'll take care of them." Aedan headed into the dining area.

"I've been thinking." Reece leaned closer. "Maybe you should only help me in the kitchen. Won't our guests think it odd that you're not from Eire? I mean, they come all this way and get served by an American?"

"I don't kno—"

"You certainly look Irish with your pretty red hair."

"I have practiced speaking with an accent." Having an Irish dad helped, even though the vast majority of the time he spoke without the brogue.

Reece rolled his eyes. "I really doubt our customers would want to hear a fake acc—"

"Aw, ye don't give a wee doll any credit."

His eyes widened and he jerked backward. "I—Iona? Have...have you been scamming us all this time?"

"What? No. Reece. What are you talking

about?" The hair on the back of her head prickled.

"With your Irish voice. I saw Iona." His face went slack as if in shock.

"Okay. This is really weird. I thought I sort of looked like her. You're talking like I'm a—"

"An exact duplicate. Aye. I didn't see it like I do now. Aedan must be…"

Her heart sank. "What?"

"Nothing."

"No. Tell me before he gets back."

He shook his head.

"Well, could you at least take me to see her? Do you know where she lives? Where she works? I'm getting really weirded out like I'm related to her. Like she's my sister."

"More like your twin."

"Just from hearing my voice with an accent?"

"It's disturbing, that."

"I thought Aedan was pulling my leg when he said I looked exactly like his ex."

Reece's puzzled glance shifted to her legs. "What now?"

Aedan returned to the kitchen with the family's order and couldn't imagine what must've taken place when he was gone. Reece grabbed the paper from him, read the order, and began preparation for it while muttering under his breath. Greta looked like she'd lost her last friend but seemed to cheer up when he asked her to help serve coffee and orange juice.

Greta had arranged her hair in a pony tail that swayed when she walked. The white apron she wore only emphasized her petite figure in her rose colored dress. She turned and caught him taking a gander at her hair as she picked up the coffee pot.

"Your hair is pretty like that."

She smiled, but she still seemed a bit unglued. "Thanks. I was hoping to go for the professional waitress look."

"You look the part." He nodded and motioned to her paintings that were displayed. "You're so talented. What I tried to say before is that I wish you could paint more. Maybe you could even include a price."

"You mean to sell?"

"Yesterday a gentleman from the States wanted to know if they were for sale. I told him I'd ask you."

"Oh, my. I guess we could. But I thought they'd serve as decorations for O'Riain's."

"While I have a chance. Could I buy the pine marten painting? I feel like it belongs here. Once it was in place, I wanted it to stay."

She shook her head, and he couldn't understand the sadness he felt over losing the painting.

"I don't want any money for it. I want you to have it." Her face looked up into his. "It's my gift to you."

Tears sprung to his eyes, surprising him by their sudden appearance. Why did she have the power to turn him into a baby? At least tears weren't gushing out, but his eyes were wet. It wasn't like him at all to be emotional over a gift. But this was different. It was something she created. Something that she thought she'd never be able to do again.

"Thank you. It means a lot…to me."

Blast. Her eyes had tears too. He mustn't let himself get tied to her. She was leaving in little over a week. But it was too late for that. He was already fond of her and falling deeper each day. He wanted to spend as much time with her as possible. "This Sunday would you like to do some sightseeing after church? Since you have precious few days you need to—"

"I'd love to. You decide where. Okay?"

He nodded, dumbfounded. He was used to Iona telling him how things would be done, when, and where. All said with much frustration and heavy sighing. Then Greta came, traveled by herself to somewhere she'd never been, and lets him decide her vacation with a trusting smile. "You're a mysterious woman, Greta."

"Aye, right." She swatted at his arm with one of Ma's cleaning cloths.

Breakfast over; Greta left the kitchen for her time off, saying she was going to work on something. Shortly after, Ma appeared with a new hire that she was showing around. Aedan recognized the youth from church as Ma introduced them. He'd be as good a worker as any. Ma shooed Aedan and Reece out of the kitchen to take a break.

Reece stepped out of the room for two seconds. "There. That's a good break."

"You go outside." Ma put her hands on her hips.

Reece looked up to the ceiling and shook his head. "I'll be back in fifteen."

"I'll be back in forty-five." Aedan headed toward the stairs.

He intended to see Greta's creative talent first hand, but then decided she might prefer quiet. Instead he picked up a key to a fourth floor room located by the stairs, far away enough from Greta's room that he shouldn't bother her.

Changes needed to be made and his executive decision put a little bounce in his step. He'd lived with his father's things in his bedroom far too long. He hurried to his room and picked up a couple of stacked boxes. The one on top had no lid and revealed some framed pictures of his parents. They used to be Ma's favorites, but she didn't want to see them anymore.

After several trips were made, the space started to look better. Why hadn't he thought of this before? He headed out of his room with a framed print under each arm when Ma came in the front door.

"What's this?" She motioned to what he carried.

"I've had it long enough. I'm moving it to a room on the top floor."

"Good."

"I still don't understand why you don't want to see all of—" Somehow her reaction seemed familiar. Ma giving up everything she loved was like Greta giving up her painting ability. Could losing a loved one to death cause that? He didn't think so. His ma was sentimental. He imagined her keeping everything in place as it was. "Why don't you want this stuff anymore?"

She shrugged and gave a small frown.

"It seems you'd want Da's things close by. Not thrown away."

Her eyes avoided his and her lip trembled. "It's too hard for me to tell you."

He set the framed pictures down. "What happened? What's this about?"

"After your da passed, old Mrs. Savage came over with her ratty jewelry and sat down to have a talk."

"Why? What'd she say? You know you can't trust her. She's the biggest gossip in all of Angel's Hollow. If there were more like her, we'd have to change the name to Devil's Hollow."

"Aedan." She said his name in a scolding tone.

"Blast it all, you know it's true."

"It was an affair. Your da had an affair with the Lynch woman." She let out a sob and tears sprung from her eyes. "I'd promised myself I'd never tell you."

His next breath stopped mid-inhale as if he'd been socked in the gut. He lowered his head and forced in air. "No. It can't be true. He was a good man. How can you believe Mrs. Savage?"

"I don't want to, but that's what she told me. Said she'd heard it right from Lynch's lips."

"Did you talk to Mrs. Lynch?"

"No."

"That would be the place to start. You're a good judge of character. You could see if Mrs. Lynch was telling the truth. We could have our favorite things back again and not live with blank walls anymore." He picked up the pictures.

A faint smile from Ma gave him a flutter of hope.

"Well. I'm still taking everything upstairs."

She moved aside, so he could go through the door and patted him on the back. "You're a good son. I hope someday you'll have a good Christian wife."

"Me, too."

As he walked through the hallway and up the stairs, Greta's image came to him. It was too much to hope for her being the one. If only she planned on staying.

But that didn't detour Reece. He was still after her, whispering to her every chance he had, offering her tastes of his cooking. Why did Reece have to cause him so much trouble? Did he try to win Greta's heart just because he could?

Chapter 11

Greta's stomach tightened as Reece stepped toward her after ending a phone call. Several days had passed since she'd told him she wanted to see Iona, and he'd tried to get information on her whereabouts from a friend. From the kitchen entrance, she could see Aedan standing at a table taking a dinner order. Her heart tugged at the sight of him.

Reece pulled her to a corner away from Aedan's line of vision. "Well, I finally found out something. She's working at a pub, and we can go and see her there tonight."

"Where is it?"

"Conk Pass. It'll take about an hour to get there.

Sure you want to go?"

"Yes, but what about Aedan?"

"What about him? It'd be better if he didn't know. Stir up a bunch of bad memories, it would. Plus he wouldn't like it if he knew I were taking you to a pub in Conk Pass."

"Is it safe enough?"

"Eh." He lifted a shoulder. "The place she works is called The Wounded Weasel. Does that sound safe to you?"

"No."

"Well, there you go. Still want to see her?"

"Yes. But I don't like the idea of leaving Aedan out of the loop."

"It's for the best. Oh, here he comes." He stepped away from her but not before Aedan saw them standing too close to each other.

****

Greta pulled her sweater together and fastened several buttons. The night air rushing in the side windows refreshed her, but her teeth wanted to chatter. Being nervous didn't help. And the guilt of it all, she couldn't dodge that. If only she'd caught up to Aedan to talk to him, but Reece found her at the stairs and hurried her along.

She tried to calm down and prayed for safety. Her heart threatened to pound out of her chest at the thought of meeting Iona—her possible twin.

Being separated from her sister could've

happened all too easily. Her mother became pregnant and sometime during the pregnancy broke up with the guy. Then later her mom met her dad and fell in love. When she gave birth, the biological father showed up and demanded to have custody of the baby, not knowing there were twin girls. She tearfully gave up one of the babies and kept the other one hidden close to her under a blanket. Then she left for home, back to America with her new husband and one baby girl.

Greta sighed and willed her eyes to not tear up. Her imagination really liked to work overtime.

"You're quiet over there," Reece said.

"It's not every day you meet your twin sister and find your biological father."

"I suppose not."

She watched the passing countryside shrouded in darkness. If only Aedan were taking her. How much more safe and comforting that'd be.

"It will be over soon. We're almost there."

Rain hit the windshield in big drops. She jumped in her seat, and Reece turned on the windshield wipers.

"That surprised me, too. It's bucketing down, isn't it?" He turned to her and grinned. "Don't worry. It will be okay."

She tried to put on a brave smile and nodded.

The car navigated around a bend and a village appeared. Spots of light glowed from windows and signs. The headlights and tail lights of the cars shone on the wet road. He parked the car on a side street and pointed to a sign hanging from a building several businesses away. The Wounded Weasel.

The lettering on the wooden sign appeared in a tattered style and a white, scruffy, cartoon weasel stood on its hind legs while leaning on a cane. One arm was in a red sling and one eye covered by a black eye patch. Its remaining eye was extremely beady, and the animal had a nasty sneer on its black lips. What a great place it must be, and where did she get her sarcastic attitude?

She stepped out of the car, and the cold damp wind whipped right through her. At least it had stopped raining. A group of tattooed men in studded leather jackets looked her up and down as they sauntered by. Some of the tattoos crept along on their necks and faces, others on their knuckles.

Reece touched her elbow. "Do you want to head back?"

"Yes, but we're not going to. I have to see her."

"Okay. But take me arm and hold tight like I'm your fella."

****

Aedan paced back and forth in the living room. It wasn't any good trying to relax. He grabbed a book and headed down the steps to sit at the front desk. No one ever came at a late hour to check in, but it was better than sitting in a blank room with thoughts of a cheating father. That Lynch woman was as fine as any woman half her age. He winced. But when would Da have had the time? Oh, aye, Da could've found time, if he wanted. Aedan pushed all the bad thoughts from his mind, sat down, and opened his book.

One of their older guests came in from outside. Unsure if the man was upset or if it was the older man's usual expression, Aedan set his book aside. "Have a goodnight."

"You too." The man nodded and headed down the hall.

Back to his book, Aedan flipped the first page intent on finding out if the main character could hold onto the rope or if he was going to fall. The ledge below might save his life if he fell, but—

"Excuse me. Do you know if Greta is around?" The man had returned.

"She's not working right now."

"I know. I knocked on her door about twenty minutes ago and she didn't answer. It's kind of important. It's about her little friend, Charles Dickens."

"What—"

"I'm Finn Brody. The pine marten that she likes so much; his name is Charles Dickens." He shifted his weight back and forth in agitation.

"What happened? Is he okay?"

"I don't know. I need to talk to Greta."

"Wait here. I'll run up and get her."

Aedan hustled up the stairs and knocked on her door with a sharp rap. "Greta?"

****

Reece opened a heavy wooden door with patchy blue paint, and Greta stepped inside. Everyone at the bar turned to look at them as they walked in. The expressions the men wore were no better than the weasel's sneer on the sign. She held onto Reece's arm like her life depended on it and tried to keep her expression blank and aloof, hoping she portrayed the don't-know, don't-care attitude. He led her to a booth, and she sat across from him.

The dark atmosphere weighed heavy, causing her fear to rise up even more. The walls were glossy navy blue and decorated with an array of bore's heads over the bar. The place had a bad indistinguishable smell like something rotten. She immediately became nauseated.

"This is supposed to be a hooley, not a funeral." Reece leaned forward and touched her knee under the table.

"A party, huh? Is that what you mean?"

"You catch on fast."

"I studied."

A dark-haired, shapely waitress, snapping gum between her teeth stepped up to their table. She did a double take upon seeing Greta. "Ye look like a girl that works here."

Greta forced a smile. "I get that a lot." She glanced to Reece who kept his attention on the woman's figure.

"Ha—well, what can I get ye?"

"I'll have a Coke." Greta pressed her lips together, waiting for a snarky reply.

"Okay, love. And you?" Her eyes flicked over Reece with appreciation.

"I'll have a pint of what's on tap—you decide."
He used a sexy voice that Greta had never heard
him use before. Then he winked at the waitress.

The waitress's eyes fluttered, and her red lips
spread into a big smile. "I'll bring ye the best."

"Don't doubt it for a minute." Reece oozed
magnetism.

She smiled again and her eyes flicked over him
once more, then she turned on her heel and headed
toward the bar.

Greta coughed from choking on her own spit.
"Reece. You're the biggest flirt ever."

"Eh, just showing a little admiration, that's all."
His regular speaking voice returned.

"Is that what you call it?"

He nodded.

"Can I give you a hint?"

"I suppose." He rolled his eyes.

"If you're with a girlfriend—someone you care
about, don't talk to any other girl that way in her
presence. Or even out of her presence for that
matter."

"Why? It's harmless. It makes the fairer sex
happy."

"It wouldn't make your girlfriend happy."

He focused on her face, seeming to try to
understand. Was Reece really that dense?

The waitress reappeared, set their drinks in front
of them in quick order, and told Reece the type beer
she brought him. The name escaped Greta as a
couple of guys sitting at the bar talked loudly to
each other in slurred voices.

"Anything else?" she asked Reece, avoiding

Greta.

"Not for now." He smiled with his eyes sparkling.

She left the table once more, swiveling her hips in a short black skirt.

"See that. Great service." His line of vision wandered from the waitress's waist to her heels.

Greta sighed. What could she say?

He leaned closer. "In a rough place like this, it helps to have the people who work here like you. Do you get my meaning?"

"Right. I guess I'm the dense one here." She said sarcastically, and folded her arms across her.

"No problem, *love*." He winked.

She waved his words away.

The men at the bar continued with their brash behavior and one shoved the other. "I told ye Iona was working tonight." The two men turned and looked at Greta.

"Uh-oh." Reece gripped her hand that was resting on the table. With his other hand slipped the car keys to her and pressed them in her palm. "If it turns bad, just run to the car, get in, and lock it. I'll get there sooner or later."

"No, Reece. I won't leave you." Her pulse quickened as adrenalin pumped.

Out of her peripheral vision, a lanky figure stumbled their direction. *Dear Lord, please protect us.*

"Hey now. You move away from Iona. You started off with the wrong doll." The ginger-haired man's blood shot eyes widened, and he poked Reece in the chest with a dirty index finger as dirty as his t-shirt. The man's jeans had holes but not the stylish ones.

"I—" Reece started.

"I'm not Iona. I'm Greta."

The guy staggered backward and studied her face. Greta was surprised to see a gentleness in his expression. He wasn't the mad, fighting bulldog she'd assumed. But the spiked choker didn't do him any favors. "You're not? But what are you doing with this guy. What's his name? Aedan. You know Eel will be spittin' mad, seeing you with your ex."

"I'm not Iona." She repeated. "And this isn't…"

Reece touched her arm and shook his head. What he tried to communicate to her went over her head. He turned to the surly man. "Sorry, I guess we look like someone you know?"

He swayed as he looked from her to Reece and back again. "What kind of malarkey is this?"

"Um, no malarkey. Really." Reece kept his tone even and pleasant.

"Hey, now, what's the problem?" A female voice spoke up behind the unsteady man.

Greta turned her attention toward the voice and quit breathing. She must have completely lost it. The woman wearing a short black dress looked like a thinner, tougher version of herself. Her light blue eyes were cold and steely surrounded by heavy dark makeup. Her lips a dark plum color. Dark eyebrows furrowed in an angry manner and red hair cut in a bob shuffled back and forth as she turned her head to look at all of them.

Greta's vision became dark around the edges. She leaned forward and steadied her hand against her forehead, breathing as evenly as she could. Someone crowded next to her in the booth and put their arm around her shoulders. It was Reece.

"It's okay. Keep breathing." He whispered the words and rubbed her back.

Slowly the dark sensation went away and her vision righted. The man with the ginger hair teetered away, mumbling about one too many. The girl who had to be Iona sat across from her and Reece.

"Are you feeling better now? I'm sorry Haig thought you were me." She smiled revealing teeth that were a little bit crowded and crooked. "But I must admit we do look somewhat alike, aye?"

"Yes. Do you think it might be possible...that we're related?"

Iona tilted her head back and let out a whoop of laughter. "Aye. All the possibility in the world, love. Me da was a traveling salesman. And did he travel. But the thing is, I don't take after me da. I take after my ma."

"Me too." Greta swallowed hard. "What is your mother's name—her maiden name?"

"Buckley."

"My mom's is McDougal. Maeve McDougal." She sighed with mixed feelings of relief and sadness.

"Well, still. I'll ask me da if he knew a Maeve McDougal." She smiled and blinked. "Give me your number. And I'll give you a call."

Greta pulled a piece of paper from her purse and wrote out her name and phone number.

"I'll only be here a short time. Nine more days

to be exact." Greta took in a shaky breath and handed Iona the paper along with the pen, so she could write out her number. "Oh my goodness. I almost forgot. How could I? What's your father's last name?"

"Same as mine. Sheehan." She pointed to her writing.

"Okay. Well. That doesn't fit the name on my birth certificate."

"Mistakes happen though, now don't they? But chances are it's just a fluke that we look alike. A shenanigan of the gods." Iona twirled her hand.

"Do you mind if we compare our hands?"

Iona placed her hand on the table and Greta did the same.

"See there." Greta moved her index finger. "My index finger is longer than my ring finger." In high school, my science teacher almost fell off his chair when he noticed. Hardly anyone is like that. Out of a class of thirty, I was the only one."

Reece's forehead wrinkled, and he looked at his hand.

"The ring finger is always longer than the index finger." Greta pointed to his finger.

"I see." Iona held up her hand which wasn't like Greta's. "At least you know we aren't identical twins." She laughed. "But think of the fun we could have tricking our fellas." Her attention wavered to Reece. "But seeing who you're with, it might not be a good idea. How is Aedan anyway?" She touched her lower lip as it quivered then turned to a frown.

"Good. He's good," Reece said.

"Hold on. I'll be right back."

Reece sipped his half empty beer. Greta took a long drink of her Coke as they watched Iona head toward the back of the bar and step through a doorway.

"Did that go how you planned?" He tilted his chin toward his neck and widened his eyes.

"I didn't have any idea, so I guess the answer is no."

"Just so you know, it was a good thing it didn't work out between—oh, here she comes."

"Reece, here." Iona handed him a wad of money. "It's not all I owe Aedan, but it's part."

He gave a smile that lasted a split second, and put the currency in his pocket.

Iona focused on Greta. "I'll find out what I can.

"Thank you. But I think we're just doppelgangers. Still that's a unique thing, right?" Greta smiled, satisfied that they weren't related.

"It is indeed." Iona bobbed her head. "Well, enjoy your evening."

Reece downed his drink. "Hoppin' mad hatters. How am I going to give Aedan the money without letting him know we've seen Iona?"

****

Aedan had given up his watch at the front desk and tried to go to bed again. He leaned back and covered up. His room was much more relaxing, since moving out all of his parent's things. He'd enjoyed reading while at the front desk. Relieved to learn that the main character had enough strength left to climb up the rope, Aedan cracked opened the book to see what would happen next. Now the guy had to sneak past a brigade of terrorists. Some days were like that.

Greta must have been sleeping soundly not to answer her door. Hopefully she hadn't been working too hard on all her projects—that he wanted to see.

The front door to their home whooshed open, then clicked shut. Footfalls sounded in their kitchen. Had to be Reece. Cupboard doors opened and closed. Water ran. A short period of silence, then Reece's bedroom door clicked shut. What could he have been up to? Some sort of date?

A floorboard clunked overhead that seemed to clutch Aedan's heart, and then a protest of squeaky bedsprings as Greta got in bed nearly wrung out his very life.

He sighed, shut his book, and turned off the light. He should've known.

Chapter 12

Next day after meeting Iona, Greta glanced over at Aedan as he drove the car. He barely said two words to her the whole morning and wore a solemn, empty-eyed expression. He'd been quiet on the way to church, too, but then again his mother and Reece carried most of the conversation there and back. Something bothered him.

"So where are we going?" She dared to break the silence.

"Sightseeing." He turned his head a fraction of an inch in her direction.

Greta wracked her brain, trying to think of lively conversation. If he didn't want to talk, it would be the perfect time to tell an in-depth story.

Sadly, the only thing she could think of was last night, and she'd promised Reece she wouldn't talk about it. But that didn't mean she couldn't ask questions.

"So what happened?" The question came out before she'd fully thought it out.

"What happened, when?" His blue-gray eyes regarded her for a second then went back to the road.

"With Iona, my look-alike?"

"It didn't work out."

"Oh, yeah." Was that all he was going to say?

"Iona…"

She waited several long seconds. "What?"

"Iona went kind of crazy on me. She thought I did things I didn't do. Kind of the opposite of what happened with you and yours, now that I think about it."

Greta waited for him to continue if he wanted. She wasn't going to push him. What a pleasure to observe the foreign green countryside without the worry of driving.

"We were going to be married. Iona accused me of seeing other girls—which I never did. I kept telling her that I'd never do such a thing, but she wouldn't listen. She insisted that her friends saw me. Then one day, she blurted out that she saw me with another woman. I've never seen her more angry.

"But it didn't happen. I couldn't understand any of it." He motioned with a free hand as the other gripped the steering wheel. "I thought I'd finally gotten through to her—got her to understand that

I'd been faithful—that I'd always be faithful. Then our wedding came. Everyone came...except her."

"I'm sorry. That had to be...terrible."

"It was." He shook his head as if to shake off a bad feeling. "I guess it was for the best. That's what me family kept saying. They said it was a mismatch."

A castle came into view, disrupting her thoughts for a few seconds. "How was it a mismatch?"

He half chuckled. "Oh, so many ways. On so many levels. The biggest was she didn't have faith in God. I was sure I could get her to come around...I wonder how she be doing now."

"How awful to think you see the one you love with someone else."

Aedan pulled into a parking place then studied her, his expression solemn. Did her words anger him?

"Of course—I believe you," she said.

His countenance relaxed, and he focused beyond her.

"Since..." Greta's mouth became dry, and she licked her lips. "Since I look like her, does it bother you?"

He shook his head. "The more time I spend with you, the less I see Iona in you. I think it's mostly the color of your eyes and hair. And well, maybe your height. Your faces are similar but by no means an exact copy. I fell in love with that face, you know." His eyes became gentle with emotion, then as if he'd realized what he'd said, he looked away.

"Well, do you know where you are?" He changed the subject.

"I couldn't miss seeing the castle. Or the Blarney Castle sign." Excitement pulsed through her.

"I couldn't have you come to Ireland and leave without seeing—"

Greta looked over her shoulder at a sign with a skull and crossbones. "The Poison Garden?"

He laughed. "Well, that too. Shall we?"

She opened her door as he stepped out of the car and came around to her side. She held onto his forearm as she stepped on uneven ground, losing her balance. "Poison?" *What kind of garden would it be?*

"Are you worried now? I'll not let you be a *eatin'* any of the vegetation." He cradled her elbow with his hand and smiled.

"The poison won't travel through the air and get us?"

"Hmm?"

"You know—like the poppy field from *The Wizard of Oz.*" Could he tell that she teased him?

"What now? The American traveler...*scared* by plants?" He took a step back as he touched his beard with an index finger. "I know what to do." He took her hand and held it. "That help?"

"Aye." She nodded and smiled, glad that he continued to hold her hand as they walked.

"Mind yerself, now. No touchin', smellin', or eatin' the plants." He pointed to the sign that said basically the same thing. "And if you get too close, I'll pull you way."

"Thank you, kind sir." She bowed her head. "All teasing aside, they aren't kidding, are they?"

He shook his head. "See the purple flowered plant? Wolfsbane. It can even kill you if you touch it."

"Whoa." She shuddered.

"I guess that be why they have the more poisonous plants in cages."

"And why they have nice pathways throughout the garden. You can almost tell by looking at the Wolfsbane that there's something bad about it—that you should stay away. The flower and leaves look...alien."

"I bet all of these plants sprouted up along with the thorns after sin came into the world." He looked thoughtfully throughout the garden. "Or I guess they could've already been there and changed."

"It's almost like the result of sin, garden."

"Hence the skull and crossbones signs. The result of sin is death. So good of me to bring you here." He laughed. "Ready to go to the castle?"

"Yes—but don't think I didn't like the garden. It's very interesting in a different sort of way."

She let go of his hand to take his picture. He obliged her by making a squinty eyed expression of distaste by one of the plant signs. He took the camera to take her picture. She pressed her lips together in what she thought to be a frown.

He chuckled and then handed her the camera. "Before we go to the castle, would you like to check out the other gardens and the Rock Close? You'll be able to get shots of the castle from different angles that way."

"Sounds great." Greta loved the idea of getting more images of him and could visualize her new scrap book of her trip to Ireland.

Aedan led her through a couple more gardens then came to Rock Close.

"What is this place? Kind of like a rock garden?" Some of the trees seemed to grow right through boulders. Their roots twisting around the stony earth.

"Aye, more or less." He nodded.

"Ooh, a waterfall. The rock formations are so unusual." She motioned toward a group in rounded shapes like lava in a lava lamp.

"Let's see what's inside that cave." He said the words in an eerie higher pitch as if to scare her.

"Uh…" From where she stood, she couldn't see a thing in the dark opening.

He held back a laugh that came out in snort. She didn't know what to expect. He posed by the entrance with a big smile as he pointed to the darkness within. Another great picture.

Moving closer, she could see the walls and floor. "Stairs. Stone steps—that go down? That's kind of creepy."

"They're the wishing steps. You make a wish as you step down them."

She followed him down the steps that turned and came out to an opening lower in the garden. "What did you wish?"

"I didn't; I prayed." He smiled a slow smile.

"Oh, you're good." But as she thought about it, her wish had been a prayer, too. She'd directed it to God.

"What did you wish?"

"That I'd be able to come back to Ireland again

someday. What did you pray?"

He half closed his eyes and shook his head.

"Please? Tell me?"

He pushed his breath out in a whooshing noise. "What will you think?"

"I'm your friend, remember?"

"Okay, then…That you'd never leave."

"Wh—" Her heart filled to overflowing. Filled with what, she wasn't really sure of. Happiness? Love? Happiness and love? Relief. "Really?"

"We'll never be able to find help as good as you."

The back of her hand clunked against her forehead, and she made a crying noise to tease him in return.

He smiled and patted her on the shoulder. "There, there."

Love shone in his eyes. She was certain of it.

They made their way to the castle; the ancient rock structure took her breath away. "How amazing it would be to see it when it had just been built."

"It would be strange to call it home, to be sure."

The rough stone wall was cold to the touch. She chronicled the walk through the castle with many pictures. As they reached the top and looked down, a feeling of unsteadiness caused her to hold onto a rail. Not exactly that she was afraid of heights, it was being close to edge and looking down that bothered her.

"Quite a sight down there." Aedan leaned over the edge.

"I know. Not sure I can look."

"Are you going to kiss the Blarney stone?"

"Are you?" She tried to stand still and wondered if she was swaying back and forth.

"No, I *already* have the gift. Of gab."

"Of course." She took a hold of his arm. "I'm going to forego it this time."

"Greta, you're not going to—"

She cringed. "I'm sure it's all very fun and nice…but I'm not going to put my lips where thousands have been."

"Guess I'll have to do it then." He set his jaw.

"No." She shook her head.

"Why?" He took a step toward the long line of tourists waiting their turn.

"I can't let you." She tightened her grip on his arm.

He rolled his eyes and gave half of a laugh. "Okay, this way to the dungeon."

"The dungeon?"

He nodded and took her by the hand, leading her down the steps. They reached the main level and then proceeded down more steps. The narrow pathways revealed small rooms covered with bars.

"This is—"

"No, wait." He pulled her to a secluded outside corner. "You have to kiss the Blarney stone." His gaze bore down into her eyes.

"I won't."

"You have to. You need to have the gift. And I have to kiss the stone too."

She shook her head. "Nothing doing."

"Okay. You've made your choice then?" He took a step closer.

"What choi—"

"We have to kiss each other. It's the only way around it. You can share my gift of gab."

His gift of gab, indeed. His reasoning made her laugh inside. He was as big a tease as his brother. In answer, she closed her eyes, put a faint smile on her lips, and tilted her face towards his. She expected a quick touch of the lips just like he'd do with the Blarney stone.

He held her shoulder and one hand gently touched the back of her neck. His lips moved against hers tenderly, evoking more love with his warmth than she thought possible. His beard and mustache were a combination of roughness mixed with softness against her skin, adding to the tirade of emotions pulsing through her.

When he pulled away, she was left speechless. What happened to the gift of gab?

Chapter 13

Aedan stepped away from Greta. Why he ever got the idea of using the Blarney stone as a means to kiss her was beyond him, but he was glad he did. More than that, Greta had kissed him back. Gobsmacked over the sensation, that's what he was—totally surprised. Excitement surged through him as if he'd just awakened after a long sleep.

Several long seconds ticked by without either of them saying a word. He knew he had a silly smile plastered on his face as he studied her somewhat startled expression. She smiled back, maybe a tad bit embarrassed.

"Well now, do you have the gift of gab? Can

you feel it?" A small chuckle escaped, but he couldn't help it. Joy thrashed around on his insides.

"Oh—aye. And more pleasant than kissing a rock." She pushed his arm.

"More than a thousand lips haven't touched me either." He smiled.

"Now that be comforting, Aedan O'Riain." She used her Irish voice.

The drive back home seemed short as Aedan shared more childhood stories of himself and Reece. Greta told a few about her brother, Bart, too. He wasn't a trickster like Reece, but Bart had his own share of getting into trouble. Aedan prayed again that she could stay and never leave. Was it a selfish prayer? He couldn't determine for sure.

He held her hand as they walked in O'Riain's Cottage and planned what they could have to eat.

"After all you've done today taking me sightseeing, I don't want you to feel like you have to make dinner." Greta's side touched his as they squeezed through the door.

"I—" He stopped short losing his train of thought. Sitting in a chair in the front lobby was Finn Brody. "Greta, Mr. Brody wants to see you. I'm sorry I forgot to tell you. He came looking for you last night."

How would she take the news of her little friend? It made him sick. Also he didn't need to be reminded of Reece taking her away somewhere last night.

"For what?" she said in a hushed voice.

"Here he comes. It's about the pine marten."

"Is he okay?"

"Greta, there you are. I've tried to find you last night. Aedan said that he knocked on your door, but you didn't answer—sound asleep you were. Then today—"

"Mr. Brody, I'm so sorry that I took her away without seeing you. I—"

The older man held up a hand. "Ah now, it's okay."

"What happened? Is Charles Dickens..." She shot a glance to the dining room where the pine marten's picture hung.

"I don't know if the little guy is alive or not. Remember the three langers that bothered you? The ones passing through town?"

"Wait." Upset pulsed in Aedan at a quick pace. "Three men. Were bothering you?"

"Finn got rid of them. And they were more like kids."

"Aye. But they came back in revenge. They scared poor Charles with their shouting, and he dashed out in front of a car."

"He's dead?" Her fingers covered her mouth, and her eyes turned teary.

Aedan put his arm around her shoulders and held her close, wanting to offer comfort.

"I don't think so. There was a wretched thump noise, but he turned around and headed me direction then back into the woods. I went after him and called, offering food, but he wouldn't come. I tried again today, but..." Finn blinked several times. "I was hoping you could come with me to try to find him. He'd come out for you."

"I'll come." She wiped the corner of her eyes,

then in a soft voice to Aedan said, "Will you come, too?"

****

Greta walked in silence with Aedan and Finn, heading toward the favorite bench. The pine marten was nowhere in sight. She feared the worst that the animal had run off to die. "If only he'd hurried to the woods when he was scared, instead of into the street."

"Aye. I brought some peanut butter bread. It might coax him out." Finn pulled it out of his pocket. "Let's head in the direction he ran."

"You two go on ahead. I'll keep you within sight," Aedan said. "He doesn't know me as well."

"Okay." She glanced through the ferns and taller plants as she walked to see any movement. Finn did the same. She prayed that Charles would be alive and well.

"I've grown attached to the little guy." Finn rubbed an eye.

"I understand. I feel that way, too and haven't known him as long."

They walked in silence to the woods. The hurt pine marten reminded her of The Wounded Weasel sign. Her thoughts drifted to the rough people inside the pub. It was almost as if they themselves were hurt, and that's where they ran to escape. They might not be in pain physically but seemed injured in spirit. Sadness weighed heavy on her. They, too, were people God loved, and in their trouble they ran the wrong direction. Words from the Bible came to mind. *Come to Me in your time of trouble, and I will rescue you.*

What could she do for them? Befriend them in some way…pray for them. If they could find their way to the Lord and be rescued by Him—have peace for their wounded spirit. Run the right direction in their time of trouble.

Finn stopped and she stood motionless beside him. He opened the plastic wrap and held the treat in his hand. "Charles Dickens."

"Food." She tried the word she said to him most often.

Green shrubs and plants surrounded them, along with wide-trunked trees. Definitely an older forest. A movement caught her eye. She blinked not believing what she saw and touched Finn's arm.

He looked the direction she pointed and gave a chuckle. "Bless me soul."

Charles peeked out from a tree hole. Happiness filled her and escaped in a short laugh. She glanced over her shoulder to see Aedan about a stone's throw away and motioned for him to come.

"Charles Dickens is alive?" Aedan smiled. "I can't believe those words actually came out of my mouth."

Chapter 14

Greta followed Aedan around the outer edge of the uneven pillars of Drombeg Stone Circle. Each marker she passed was like a day that had gone by—a full week, now Sunday again. The more days that passed, the more she struggled with the thought of leaving for home. Only two days.

During the last work week she'd helped Aedan and Reece serve customers, and they were the busiest they'd been yet. Aedan had taken his morning breaks with her and they spent the times talking to Finn and Charles. In the evenings they were either alone in the kitchen or off on a sightseeing expedition to see her favorite, the cliffs at Mizen Head.

She'd never forget the night they took dinner to Mrs. McFeely and Mrs. Donovan. She loved them. Mrs. McFeely with the newfangled microwave and Mrs. Donovan's cantankerous style. Each of them dear in their own way.

The night they saw a show with Irish dancers, the music stirred deep within her soul, giving her a great desire to dance. But how could she learn? There weren't classes offered back at home. And even if they were, Aedan wouldn't be there.

The hardest time of all came at the end of the evenings, saying goodnight to Aedan. He'd tried to explain why he'd only kiss her on the cheek, but it didn't help. And it didn't work. She smiled and her face turned warm. His kiss always started on the side of her face, but always ended up on her lips.

Greta leaned against one of the pillars. Aedan's footfalls crunched ahead of her on the gravel. He must've noticed that she'd stopped. He turned and took a couple of steps toward her and stood motionless. The eerie angles of the rocks surrounded them. A passing cloud blocked the warm sunshine. Wind picked up a strand of her hair and carried it across her face. She pushed it back in place and held her hair by her shoulder. Even though she'd wanted to see a stone circle, all it brought was uneasiness.

"Did you know stone circles are called thin places?" Aedan glanced beyond her then to her face.

"Thin places. I've never heard of it."

"Yes, it's like our time or—I don't know—existence of life is thin here. In ancient places like this." He motioned a circle with his arm.

"*Thin*?"

"The barrier is thin here between our world and eternity or our world and God. Do you feel an unexplained strange sensation? Sometimes I do—when I've come here before. It's like an energy or electricity."

She'd sensed it, but thought it was only her misgivings about leaving. "I...I do feel it. But I don't think it's God."

He watched her, his expression gentle. He opened his mouth to answer.

She continued, "I felt God's presence in church today, when I prayed. It's like a deep love mixed with peace. Kind of like a wonderful feeling when you're cold and covered with a warm blanket. Does that make sense?"

He nodded. "Sure do. I was about to say the same. Well, not the warm blanket part."

"Here, it isn't like that. It's different..."

Aedan folded his arms across his chest and glanced at the nearby pillars, evidently trying to figure it out.

Greta looked upward to the sky. "Maybe we are sensing the unseen powers in the heavenly realms, the fight between good and evil."

"And they picked this spot to have it out?"

"Well, when you put it that way." She smiled and pressed her hands against the cold, gray stone. "Maybe it is the angle of the stones and how they look. It's not something we see every day. The light bounces off the edges, planes, and corners then the gravity from the boulders pulls at us. That's enough to make anyone feel funny."

"Aye, right." He rolled his eyes in a disbelieving manner. "Still it be a strange feeling, that." His hand rested on the rock next to hers. "If we had time, we could do a whole expedition of stone circles and structures. There are so many of them in Ireland. And another trip for seeing castles."

"Don't forget the all of the shoreline cliffs, especially Mizen Head."

"I'd love to put together trips like that. Just think if you were—"

"Aedan. That's so perfect and right. You should offer planned guided trips to your guests. Take them to all the best places. You could even have the excursions follow a theme just like you said. It would draw people to O'Riain's Cottage."

"You think it could work?" His eyes lit up. "I like it. I like it a lot."

Heaviness tugged at her. She stepped away from the stone and clasped her hands together. If only she could see the plan come to fruition. Footfalls on gravel crunched closer. She looked at her fingernail polish where a spot had chipped off. Her emerald green skirt of her dress flowed gently in a breeze. Aedan stood close, the tips of his shoes almost touching hers. He held her arms and she focused on his blue and black checked shirt. Slowly, she lifted her eyes to his face. Would he ask her to stay?

He smiled at her then stepped away. "We should go, so we can go see—"

"I know. But first..." She looked in her purse for her camera and pulled it out.

He kept his smile, folded his arms across his

chest, and leaned toward the tall pillar.

"No, that's all wrong. Remember? This is a mysterious place."

He frowned and furrowed his brows. "That better?"

"Yes." She stood beside him, getting them both in the picture. She flipped the camera over to see the result. They'd make a good couple. He wore a worried look on his face, and her expression showed a deflated feeling.

Aedan drove the car through the countryside to Cork City, and they approached the outskirts of town. Greta became more nervous the closer they got to the house of the man with the same last name as her birth certificate.

"Thanks for helping me with this."

"Are you doing okay?" he asked.

She nodded. "But can we do something fun after this?"

"No problem. Reece is making chocolate pies. How does that sound?"

"Fantastic."

"Then we can watch a movie back at my place." He thrust a thumb to his chest.

She smiled. "Thanks. Have any Irish romantic comedies?"

"We do." His voiced turned mock forlorn. "Ma made sure of it."

When they arrived at the address, she noted the small red house with a thatched roof appeared deserted. The lawn and flower garden were overgrown. "Oh, dear. I think I know why no one answered the phone."

"Just the same. Let's go see."

He held her hand as they walked up to the worn wooden door and knocked. No answer.

"Well. I could try again, next Sunday for you." He held her hand tighter as they turned back to the car.

Chapter 15

Tuesday morning came. Greta's plane ticket information lay on her bed along with her phone. She'd prayed to make the right decision and thought for certain she'd have a specific answer, but none was forthcoming. What should she do? She paced the floor, picked up the phone then set it back down again on the bed.

She stepped to the window and watched people walk by on the sidewalks below. This place had become her home. She loved Aedan, and leaving him was impossible. Her gut told her she shouldn't give up. They needed a chance to see if their future was with each other.

Reece and Alice came into sight. His mother

supervised as he positioned the chalkboard sign. Finn was next to appear. She smiled, half expecting him to be carrying Charles. Finn headed off toward the direction of his bench. She'd grown fond of him and the pine marten. It was like he was an adopted uncle and Reece and Alice were extended family. She cared about them. How could she go on with her life like they didn't exist?

What of her job back in Indiana? And her dad and brother? A stab of guilt jolted her. She'd forgotten to reply to her dad's emails or even check them recently. It'd be okay. She'd either see him tomorrow or send him an email to explain. Somehow she couldn't bear to hear his voice. It would make her feel even more torn. She loved her dad and brother so much.

She'd assumed God would give her a peace with an answer of what direction to take. The interior of Aedan's church came to mind. She was at home there and felt at peace. Aedan had sat on one side of her and Mrs. McFeely on the other. She'd leaned over to tell of her prayers for Mrs. Donovan. If Greta left, she'd never see Mrs. McFeely again. Greta wanted to see the older lady's happiness when Mrs. Donovan finally agreed to go to church with her. Hopefully it would happen soon.

What it all boiled down to was that Greta loved them all. She wanted to help Aedan on his endeavors. She wanted to be a part of his life.

She turned away from the window and picked up the phone. As she gripped it in her hand, it rang. Iona.

****

Aedan wrestled with his thoughts as he worked. How could it be Greta's last day? How could he let her go? Would it be right to plead with her to stay? She had a successful job in the States, family, and friends. How could he ask her to give it all up for him? O'Riain's Cottage had been doing better financially the last couple of weeks but how could the money compare? Then again, Greta seemed happy with simple things. Being able to stay in the small room on the fourth floor proved as much.

He prayed God would find a way for Greta and him. He'd promised her he'd follow her to the airport and say goodbye. His stomach churned with the thought. He didn't want his eyes to sprout tears.

He put the last dirty dish from the noon meal in the dishwasher. As he turned on the washer and thought of the water clearing everything bad away, he wished it could be the same for his thoughts. He needed a clear direction.

Then he knew. He couldn't let her go. He wouldn't.

The other problem bothered him, too—he'd meet it head on.

Reece stepped in front of him. "You've been quiet."

"Well—"

"Ma and the intern are takin' over for a while. I'm goin' to—"

"Great. At least for an hour or two?"

Reece nodded and covered a yawn. "I'm going

to grab a few winks."

"I'll be back. A few things need tending."

Aedan headed off to the car, grabbing the phonebook on the way. He had to see the Lynch woman. He gritted his teeth even thinking about her. As he sat behind the wheel, he opened the phonebook and found her name. The hair on the back of his neck prickled. He'd had a general idea of where she lived, but the address was too close for comfort.

When he pulled up to the swank, blue house with white shutters, a curtain shifted. Lynch was home. Before his courage failed him, he moved swiftly out of the car, up the walk, and knocked on her front door.

The door opened revealing an auburn-haired, model. Or at least she could've been. For being at least twenty years his senior, Lynch seemed even more striking than the last time he'd glimpsed her at an open-air market.

A red fingernail touched an equally red lip. "You're one of the O'Riains." Eyelashes fluttered over hazel eyes. "I remember."

"Aedan O'Riain. Could you spare a minute?"

She motioned with a tilt of her head for him to enter. He hated to step inside, but the topic wasn't something for anyone passing by. *Lord, help me.*

A few minutes of answered questions and his feet stepped back through the door to freedom. He glanced at his watch, and adrenalin pumped as his mind whirled with the next task.

****

Aedan had two minutes before he needed to head back down to work, and he placed one of the favorite large paintings above the couch. Ma would either be terribly pleased…or not. He stood at the center of the living room and observed his handiwork while taking in a large satisfied breath. Their home looked so much better.

He headed down the stairs as his mother headed up. They stopped on the landing.

"Ma, there be a surprise for you."

"What? I hope it be a good surprise and not a bad one."

"Good. It be good." He paused before he plunged ahead. His ma wouldn't like the idea of where he'd just been. "I saw the Lynch woman. She had nothing to do with Da. Lynch didn't know how Mrs. Savage got the idea that there was an affair. So…there you are. Da was innocent."

"You wouldn't be telling me a story to spare me feelings?" Her eyes pierced him to see any falsehood.

"It's the truth. She be tellin' the truth. She thought the idea of her and Da to be quite hilarious."

An unwelcome image of the woman came to him. Lynch had titled her back and laughed a horrid garbled sound with her earrings bobbing back and forth like miniature yo-yos. She said that she hadn't even as much as talked to his father. Her eyes had flicked over Aedan as she said she went for younger men. Made him feel like hurling his partially digested lunch at her before he stepped out the door.

"The best news, that is." His ma smiled and put

a hand over her heart.

"Well, go on now and see the surprise." Aedan motioned up the steps.

Her smile grew and a little bounce was in her step as she headed up the stairs. She'd love to see all of the treasured things of their home back in place. How tragic it would've been if everything had been thrown out the way she'd wanted. One mistruth had disrupted their lives for close to a year.

How important it was to be faithful. He touched a newly purchased Claddagh ring through his shirt pocket. *Greta.* He'd plead with her to stay before she left for the plane. He'd give her the Irish ring of promise.

****

Greta sat in her room, half dazed by Iona's phone call. Everything had been neatly tied up with Iona not being related and now there was a question again. Iona's father had known someone by the name of Evie McDougal, but he was a little unsure of the name. Her mom could have gone by Evie. The time of year and place all matched up. The only way to know for sure would be to check with her dad to see if he knew anything.

She could hear herself telling Aedan. "Oh, by the way. Iona and I are half sisters." What would he say?

If that wasn't enough, she'd made a life-changing decision without even a call to her father or brother; she'd only sent them a short line of an email. They probably thought she was crazy by not taking her flight, but she couldn't even imagine the torment she'd feel if she were on a plane back home.

As for her job at home, it was a done deal after a phone call giving her resignation. She had to be quite the topic of the day—three weeks of vacation and not coming back. Her boss probably had a line of people to take her place. She'd not foreseen that she'd be upset over the decision.

She couldn't understand her feelings or even find a way to explain.

Aedan. Her heart missed a beat. What did he think? She'd only spoken to him briefly at dinner and told him she'd see him in the morning. As far as he knew, she was taking a later flight than she'd planned. Things seemed so messed up.

Instead of a joyful excitement she had anticipated, she worried. Her head pounded. What if Aedan disapproved of her staying and working at O'Riain's? No, she wouldn't go there. That was completely off target from what was real. They had something...wonderful.

She made herself comfortable in bed, willing bad thoughts away. Rest and prayer would do some good. If only she could relax and understand she'd made the right decision.

When she heard a sharp voice, she blinked her eyes open to darkness. Not again. She hadn't meant to fall asleep. The male voice said something urgent,

"Why are you waking me up? I've got to get

sleep." Aedan's voice.

"Come on now! What I'm telling you is important. Iona is really stirred up. I don't know what kind of trouble's going to happen, or what she's going to pull." Reece's voice raised in upset.

"What?"

"I have to tell you before you hear it from her. I'm sorry, brother. There wasn't any other way." He paused. "I...it was me."

"What are you talking about?"

"Iona's friends. They saw me with a girl— more than one girl. They thought I was you."

"And you didn't set them straight?" Disbelief came through in Aedan's voice.

"When I had that time off for cookery training, I didn't go. I went to Cork City. I grew in the rest of my beard that I'd started, and I wore clothes like yours. I became you. I made sure Iona saw me with—"

"Reece. *Why?* You ruined my reputation? You broke us up? I can't—" The words were fraught with pain. A shuffling noise sounded, a guttural growl, and a thud. Had Aedan pushed Reece into a wall? "You ruined my life!"

"Please try to understand. She was bad for you. She hurt you. You weren't the same. It was like you were half alive. Don't you see?"

"I don't." His voice rumbled with anger. "Just go." A pause of silence then door clicked shut.

Greta couldn't fathom what Aedan must be feeling. Had it changed his feelings toward Iona? A sob caught in her throat. Wait. He'd said Iona wasn't right for him on many levels. He'd moved on. Greta had to hold onto that. Yeah, she held onto it like a tiny life preserver while bobbing on ocean waves. *God, please help.*

And sleep? Totally out of the question. She tried to get comfortable again.

After what seemed like hours but had to be minutes, she sat in bed, then crept out of her room. On stealth mode, she slipped down the stairs, to the dining room, heading to the kitchen. Reece had set aside a piece of chocolate pie for her in the refrigerator. If there was any time that she needed chocolate, it was now.

She stepped by the back door. Moonlight streamed in its window. A movement outside caught her eye and her heart sank. Aedan stood with Iona who gestured with her hands as she talked. She brushed the outside corners of her eyes as she cried. Iona slipped her hands around him and they embraced in a kiss.

Greta tore away from the scene and hurried back up to her room, tears flying away from her face as she went. Her stomach cramped with nausea. Iona was his first real love. He'd intended to marry her. She was the one with whom he had a past. Greta had to leave; it was the only thing to do. How could she stand in Iona's way?

In her room, she hastily threw things into her bags, then carefully took the items off her bulletin board and tucked them away in her suitcase. She held the card from Mom. *I'll always love you.*

Greta would have to leave the empty board behind. No use to take it with her anyway. Her mom's words came to mind. "Go to Cork," her eyes had beckoned. Greta looked at the simple framed board, tears stinging her eyes as she held the little kitten card. Mom was telling her to go the corkboard to see the card and to remember that she'd always love her.

She doubled over, holding the card. It was all so clear. Mom *hadn't* intended for her to come here. There was no way to find her biological dad with the old Irish name, even if he still lived in Ireland. Aedan didn't need her.

At least with her coming, he'd come to find out how his relationship with Iona had been manipulated. No wonder Reece wanted the mistake of being called Aedan to be overlooked when they were at The Wounded Weasel. His body language during the incident made complete sense now.

She washed her face, set out a few things for the O'Riain family, and rested for a while. She'd leave when there wasn't any chance of running into Aedan. It would spare him having to explain that he wanted his first love. It would spare her, too. She didn't want to hear it.

Chapter 16

Aedan woke up to a knock on his door and his mother's voice. "You've overslept."

"What?" *Oh, no.* "Sorry. I'll be right down."

"Hurry, get dressed and come with me."

"Why?"

No answer from Ma. Was she still in the hallway? Typical. He jammed on his pants in a hurry and thrust on a shirt. What other kind of drama would there be today? He stepped out of his bedroom, and she still gave no explanation.

He walked with her out of their home apartment and broke out in a sweat when they went upstairs. "For the sake of all that's fair, tell me what's going on."

She shook her head with a frown. "Go see for yerself. Greta's room."

His heart thudded. "Is she okay?"

She shook her head.

He raced up the steps and slipped on one, falling to his knees. He righted himself and ran the rest of the way and knocked on her door. It moved with his touch. A sliver of reflected light shown from the room. As he pushed the door completely open, prickles of shock raced down his spine. The room had been vacated. An empty corkboard stood against the wall. Papers occupied the round table. He moved closer to see, but his eyes blurred. What happened?

A design for a menu lay on the table. Celtic lettering proclaimed the name O'Riain's and a pine-martin sat in a green forest. Clovers decorated the edge. Perfect. Another paper listed a web address and information where ads were placed. *Bless her heart.*

But where was she? He gulped and looked around at the empty room, hoping she'd appear. Then he noticed a note on the pillow. He picked up the paper and read her words explaining why she had to leave.

"No…" He shook his head. "That's *not* right. How could this have happened?"

In a daze, he folded the note and stashed it in his pocket. The menu and information he tucked under his arm and put it in his room on the way down the stairs.

As he walked by the front desk, a distinguished, professional looking man stopped him. He was a tall, broad-shouldered, older man with brown hair and a weary expression. "Excuse me. I'm looking for Greta Conner. I'm her father."

"Oh, you're Padraig O'Cnaimhin?"

The older man blinked. "I haven't heard that name in a very long time, but yes, I go by Craig Conner."

The news him between the eyes. *Oh, Greta.* Her biological father was the one who raised her.

Chapter 17

Days later, Greta stood with her dad in the living room of her childhood home. She didn't feel up to talking. She'd made a fine mess of things—of everything. But how could she have known that her dad changed his name to a more easily pronounced English name when he came to America with her mom?

"Dad, it would've helped if you told me about the name on the birth certificate."

"I tried. I said not to worry about the name. That it was right."

In spite of herself, she half smiled. "But you didn't tell me it was *you*."

"That's what I meant." He hugged her and she

hugged him back. "I never meant for you to be hurt."

Greta stepped out of the embrace. "Just to make sure…Mom wasn't involved with a man named Sheehan about nine months before I was born?"

"Definitely not." A stunned look flitted across his face. "Why would you ask that?"

"Because I met a would-be twin when I was there…but—"

"Greta, your mom and I were faithful to each other. We waited for marriage. It's a shame this generation can't see the value in that."

"I see it."

"So you ran into someone who looked like you?"

"Aedan's ex-girlfriend." Greta pushed back her hair, not wanting to talk about it. How could she, when her dad's girlfriend had stepped into the living room, took one look, and left the room. But Greta needed to let her ill feelings toward Joanie go away. The poor lady did try.

"Aedan was really broken up about you leaving. He doesn't understand."

She sighed. "I never should've gone there." Footfalls by the front door bothered her. What was Joanie doing? Hushed voices whispered in the background. Had she invited a friend over?

"All I did was mess things up. I made you worry and caused you to go on a wild goose chase. I'm sorry. I'm glad you're back home." Greta hugged him a good long while then released him. His eyes softened, showing concern and love. "I thought Mom wanted me to go there, but she didn't. She was telling me to go to the corkboard to look at a card and remember her." Her voice trembled. "Not go to Cork."

"Greta, but what about who you met there? You wouldn't have met Aedan. He cares for you. While I was there, I got to know him. He's a good man—a good Irishman." He smiled and she caught that he compared Aedan to himself.

"What can I do?" She paced to a window. "Go back? How do I know…if he wants me there?"

"Greta." A voice came from behind her. A familiar male voice.

She turned and couldn't believe if what she saw was real. Tears surprised her by springing to her eyes.

"Aedan." She lost her breath as he came near and held her. "You're…you're here."

"I am. You know, Indiana is the same size as Ireland, so no big deal." He chuckled and Dad joined in.

"Well, I'll leave you two alone, so you can catch up. Great to see you, Aedan." Dad slapped him on the back in a friendly gesture and stepped out of the room.

"I heard what you said." His voice turned quiet and husky. "You're wrong."

"Wrong?" She studied his expression, and he held both her hands.

"Your ma did tell you to go to Cork."

She shook her head as he nodded.

"Aye, she did. God used those words to bring you to us, to bring you to me."

Greta waited as he struggled to put his thoughts

into words.

"Reece…" Aedan paused and took a breath. "I didn't understand what Reece was doing, but he meant only to help me. He told me that he prayed for someone like you to come, and he did his best to get me to wake up and live my life.

"Reece wasn't the only one who prayed. Ma prayed for a miracle—for more customers." He smiled. "And your amazing talent brought them to us. Finn Brody said that he prayed for a caring friend…who would show him that there are still good people in the world."

Greta's heart ached. She loved them, all of them. But most of all her love for Aedan made her feel like she could burst.

"I—prayed." He gave her hands a gentle squeeze. "Remember the wishing steps?"

She gave a short nod.

"I love you, Greta." He softly touched her cheek.

She couldn't catch her breath. Aedan loved her as much as she loved him? Her heart pounded. She placed her hand over his and titled her head into his palm.

"And I *pray*—that your feet will take you where your heart is," he whispered as his eyes looked into hers.

Tears of heated emotion threatened. Her heart did belong with him, his Irish heart. She wanted Ireland to be her home more than any other place. Gently, she moved his hand away. "But what about Iona? I saw—"

"What did you see?"

"You kissed—"

"I didn't. She came to apologize and tried to bring back feelings between us. She'd learned that it was Reece who pretended to be me and was the one seen dating all the girls. I told her Reece was right to split us up—*God help me*." He closed his eyes as if adding more to a silent prayer. "Greta, it's you I care about. You that my heart belongs to." He whispered, "You that I love. I'd planned to beg you to stay, to not get on the plane. But when morning came—"

He slipped his hand to an inside pocket of his jacket and pulled out a ring designed with two hands holding a heart with a crown. "This is for you. It's the Claddagh promise ring; it stands for my love, friendship, and loyalty. It's yours—no matter your answer—but will you…come back with me?"

His gaze didn't waver from her face. He seemed to hold his breath with a resolved yet tortured look in his eyes.

"Yes," she said with a nod and a smile she couldn't hold back.

He sighed with relief. "Whew. You scared me there for a minute."

She held out her left hand for him to slip on the ring.

"It's for your right hand." He slipped it on her finger as she admired the Irish ring. He squeezed her left hand and let go.

Then reached in the pocket once more and got down on one knee. A beautiful, sparkling diamond ring in his hand. "Greta, will you become engaged to me? Will you marry me?"

Before she realized what she was doing, she let out a gasp. His face saddened as if he expected the answer to be no. She lost her voice, but happiness from deep within welled up in her. He had to see it; his expression broke into a smile.

"Yes." Tears of joy clouded her vision. "I love you, Aedan. I can't imagine life without you."

He slipped the diamond ring on the finger of her trembling left hand, then stood and embraced her, his kiss making everything around them melt away.

Greta was unsure of the passage of time when Aedan pulled away. He leaned close again and hugged her. "Well, we should tell your da. Will he be upset at your move to Ireland?"

"I wouldn't be surprised if he and my brother would want to live there, too. I know, at least, that they'd visit." A question niggled in the back of her mind. "Speaking of family. What is your mother's real name?"

"What?" Puzzlement wrinkled his forehead. "Are you thinkin' that she's not my ma?"

She shook her head. "If her first name isn't Alice, then…"

His incredulous expression deepened.

"Reece told me her name wasn't Alice. That she liked different nametags to wear."

"Ah—Reece." He chuckled. "Her name *is* Alice. She does like different nametags though, but they all have the name, Alice."

That thumping flat tire. "Aedan O'Riain. What are we in for?"

"Mi daza—Greta O'Riain. The best years of our lives.

81560335R00094

Made in the USA
Lexington, KY
17 February 2018